THE HOLISTIC CREATOR

THE HOLISTIC CREATOR

THE INSCRUTABLE PARIS BEAUFONT™ BOOK 8

SARAH NOFFKE

MICHAEL ANDERLE

DISRUPTIVE IMAGINATION

Copyright © 2021 LMBPN Publishing
Cover copyright © LMBPN Publishing
A Michael Anderle Production

LMBPN Publishing
PMB 196, 2540 South Maryland Pkwy
Las Vegas, NV 89109

Version 1.00, October 2021
Version 1.01, October 2021
eBook ISBN: 978-1-64971-963-8
Print ISBN: 978-1-64971-964-5

THE HOLISTIC CREATOR TEAM

Thanks to the JIT Readers
Diane L. Smith
Veronica Stephan-Miller
Deb Mader
Dorothy Lloyd
Dave Hicks
Zacc Pelter
Jackey Hankard-Brodie
Angel LaVey

If I've missed anyone, please let me know!

Editor
The Skyhunter Editing Team

To Aunt Kate—I hope to grow up to be just like you, although I've given up on actually growing up (figuratively or literally).

— Sarah

To Family, Friends and
Those Who Love
to Read.
May We All Enjoy Grace
to Live the Life We Are
Called.

— Michael

CHAPTER ONE

Zhuang Alley was where you could find the worst of the worst in the magical world. It was also where only the most rebellious tooth fairies would dare to venture. Being discovered there was one of the few reasons for expulsion from Loose Teeth College.

Courtney Montgomery banged her broken wand on a dirty trashcan with a grunt and shook her head. Her dark pigtails hit her in the face from the movement. "It still doesn't work. That old witch stole my money and gave me nothing."

Sidney laughed and twisted her nose ring around absentmindedly. She was always playing with the jewelry. "She gave you what you paid for. Nothing much. You're the dimwit if you thought that any magic spell would fix your wand."

"Shut your face, Sid," Courtney spat, ready to chuck her wand in the trash but not entirely ready to give up hope yet. She blew out a frustrated breath, making her bangs fly up off her forehead. "It's not like I had the money to waste. I'm pretty much broke at this point and with a stupid freaking broken wand too..."

"Now you're like the rest of us and a poor tooth fairy in training, without your trust fund," Sidney teased, poking her tongue out at her.

"Yeah, that wretched halfling blabbed, as I knew she would,"

Courtney seethed. "Once it came out that there was a Montgomery at Loose Teeth College, my mother cut my money faster than she could demolish a hot fudge sundae."

"Poor, without a wand, and contracted with the tooth fairies for the next several years." Sidney clicked her tongue and shook her head, appearing to enjoy her friend's plight. "Things really can't get any worse for you."

"At least I'm not ugly like you," Courtney spat.

Sidney laughed coldly. "That's the best insult you got? That's pathetic."

"You're pathetic," Courtney countered.

"You're both pathetic," Whitney threatened from the shadows, the white streaks in her black hair catching the ambient light. "Look, the shop is emptying. We can get in there soon."

"I don't get why you think this will help," Courtney complained, continuing to flick her wand and quietly complain about its brokenness.

"Because this will get me into Happily Ever After College," Whitney explained. "Or soon to be called, Unhappily Ever After College." She giggled with evil delight.

"You sure this guy can forge you new records?" Sidney asked, her attention focused on the dark shop with dirty windows. "Ones that will make you not look like a fairy with a criminal background and a menace to society?"

Whitney nodded, twirling her long hair around her finger. "Yeah, he says he can, and I have the requirements for getting into Happily Ever After College with me. I'll have the guy tailor it to that."

Courtney sighed, putting her useless wand in the waistband of her black tutu. "Yeah, Mother was livid when she found out that Saint Valentine was allowing Headmistress Willow to open up enrollment to non-fairies. Apparently, that halfling demon witch was good for something, and now there's an initiative toward inclusivity of other races into Happily Ever After College."

Whitney grinned. "Can you imagine how messed up things will be when fairy godmothers aren't fairies? It's stupid."

Sidney scoffed at her. "You were a magician who was going to be a tooth fairy."

"I still am going to be one," Whitney argued. "That's different because we're a class of rejects and misfits to start with. The fairy godmothers are always perfect and refined, but they don't know the slippery slope they're going down. Without our help, they're going to ruin themselves."

Sidney rubbed her hands together greedily. "But we *are* going to help."

"Yes, their intent to progress in new directions opens the doors to our attacks," Whitney stated. "Soon I'll be a student at Happily Ever After College, and from inside there I can do some real damage."

"How are you going to pass the entrance exam?" Courtney asked. "Becky says they give it to students on the first day, and if they don't pass, the headmistress asks them to leave. Apparently, it's a practical application of matchmaking principles."

Whitney rolled her eyes and twirled her unbroken wand in the air. "I'll do the one thing that no fairy godmother would ever do and employ dark magic from the Fang Wellspring. It's bound to get me by."

Sidney bounced her shoulders up and down, looking like she was pumping herself up for a fight. "You can use that same magic to disguise yourself. The whole plan is genius."

Whitney tilted her head and batted her eyelashes, feigning innocence. "Yep, I'll pretend to be a sweet little magician who always wanted to be a fairy godmother and create love for the world. Those goody-goodies won't know what hit them until I've unleashed real evil all around them and then blazed a path to their destruction.

"Then I'll waltz back to Loose Teeth College, where we'll all look like queens in comparison to the distraught and disadvantaged fairy godmothers." She cackled loudly, her eyes brimming with delighted contempt. "It will take them centuries to come back from this."

Sidney joined in the laughter. "If they ever recover."

"I hope they don't," Courtney seethed, not laughing. "Take my stupid sister down first. Then Mother will be sad when it ruins her precious Rebecca."

"I will if you pay me," Whitney said coldly and laughed again. "Oh, that's right. You can't. Your mother cut you off from the family fortune."

Courtney shook her head, her eyes low and filled with anger. "I don't need their money. I'll make it on my own."

"Come on. The shop is empty now. Let's go before we're spotted." Whitney grabbed her friends by their wrists and hauled them forward toward the dark shop.

The three women, two fairies and one magician, disappeared into the shop that sold forged documents and fake identities. They were one step closer to getting Whitney into Happily Ever After College. From there, she'd be a silent threat unlike any the fairy godmothers had dealt with before.

CHAPTER TWO

"Can you believe I have indexable boring tools?" Faraday hopped over a large piece of machinery in his lab and ducked his head behind a metal compartment, disappearing momentarily.

"Hardly," Paris said dryly while looking around the huge space and trying to decipher what half of the devices and objects were. "I've been up most of the night, reeling from disbelief."

"Me too!" the talking squirrel replied, not catching her sarcasm. "I mean, the bars are micro-grain carbide shanks with heat-treated steel heads!"

Paris sighed melodramatically. "Now I have to return your birthday gift."

Faraday glanced up suddenly, looking over his shoulder at her. "You got me indexable boring tools...oh, wait...you're joking, aren't you?"

"I'll get you some boring tools if you want," she teased. "Pretty much anything you can find in a Home Depot is boring to me."

Scoffing, Faraday returned his attention to what he was working on. "Please don't compare my superior, state-of-the-art scientific tools to things you can buy from a guy in an orange vest at Home Depot."

"Hey, it's not Chuck's fault that they don't sell zippity-do-dah tools with shark heads and microfiber lining at Home Depot where he works." Paris picked up a strange cylindrical object with a digital reading on the side and pretended to inspect it. She had no idea what it was or what she was looking at, or if she was holding it the right way.

Faraday sighed. "None of that is a thing, Pare. You're making things up. The indexable tools have micro-grain carbide shanks and—"

She held up her hand, pausing him. "Please, I choose to remain ignorant in these things. Do not educate me unless you want me to explain the entire lineage of the Kardashian family."

He blinked at her. "You don't know that information. Please tell me you don't…"

She flashed him a wicked smile and winked. "Only one way to find out."

"Fine, I won't explain to you anything about my tools," he retorted, then hopped off the large machinery and scampered across his lab.

"What you can tell me is what you're working on today, squirrel."

"I'm calibrating a software system that compares the algorithms of—"

Again Paris held up her free hand, interrupting Faraday. "I believe the Kardashian empire started with the late Robert Kardashian Senior and—"

Faraday stuck his paws to his ears, covering them up. "Stop. I can't learn such information. It's bound to overwrite some actual important scientific knowledge."

"Then let's try this again, squirrel. What are you working on today?"

"I'm trying to track down the maker of those drones that guarded the satellite Agent Ruby used to make phones addictive," he answered in a rush. He pulled his paws away from his ears and looked terrified that Paris might continue to tell him about the Kardashian family lineage.

She nodded, satisfied. "See, that's not so hard. You tell me what you're doing using English, and no one gets hurt."

"Or seriously annoyed," Faraday added.

"You're still pretty obsessed with finding this diabolical scientist or scientists who created those indestructible drones, huh?" Paris laid the cylindrical object down, having pretended to inspect it sufficiently.

"The fact that it's so difficult tells me that this person or organization doesn't want anyone to find them," Faraday answered. "I'm not obsessed. I have a hunch that they could do real harm based on their magitech capabilities.

"They created a signal that made cell phones addictive and had drones that dragons couldn't defeat. These aren't people who are trying to bring world peace and love to others. Agent Ruby employed them, and something tells me that they'll use their technology for whatever selfish gain they desire."

"Well, do you need help tracking them down? I can hold a screw driver and squint over your shoulder while you calibrate software systems," Paris offered.

"I'm not sure that would be of much use to me."

She shrugged. "Well, I tried."

"I think you have enough to keep you occupied with your studies and the new threat from Loose Teeth College."

Paris nodded. "Yeah, hopefully, the evil tooth fairies will leave us alone after my run-in with Courtney Montgomery, but I'm not holding my breath on that one."

"Yes, she might be extra charged up and out for revenge after having her wand broken and her family secret exposed," Faraday replied.

"Hey, it's wasn't me who revealed that a Montgomery was a reject at Loose Teeth College," Paris remarked. "That was Willow, who relayed the information to Saint Valentine, who then made it public knowledge to the board." She looked up at the ceiling and smiled with delight. "I would've loved to see Virginia Montgomery's face when everyone found out that her daughter was a misfit enrolled to become a tooth fairy."

Faraday smirked along with her. "Yes, for someone who preaches about honor and traditions and protecting the sanctity of the fairy godmothers, it doesn't reflect well on her or the Montgomery family."

Paris made her way to the lab's exit, the smell of coffee wafting from the dining hall calling her attention. "Well, maybe if Virginia spent a bit more time disciplining Courtney and a little less time sticking her nose in everyone's business, she wouldn't have a criminal for a daughter."

"You'll want to be careful, though," Faraday warned. "Not only have you made enemies of Courtney and her friends—"

"The Knees, as they're known," Paris cut in.

He nodded. "Yes, but I'm certain the other Montgomerys will be cross with you as well."

Paris snapped her fingers and swung her hand. "Oh, darn. Becky and I were starting to get along. I'd made her a friendship bracelet and everything."

"I don't think there's a world where you two could ever be friends," Faraday stated matter-of-factly. "She's a bully at her core, and your demon blood makes it so you must stamp out anyone who abuses others or has the slightest of evil intent."

"That's fine by me," Paris sang from the heavy lab door that separated Faraday's modern scientific lair from the rest of the mansion—which was the exact opposite in feel and appearance with warm wood and curvy lines. "I have enough friends and the very best ones too."

Faraday grinned at her. "Well, try to stay out of trouble, if you can…"

"I can't and I won't. You try not to blow up the college or break one of your boring tools."

"I won't, and it would be impossible because they're made of—"

Paris once more held up her hand. "I believe that Robert Kardashian Senior was married to—"

"Have a good day, Pare," the squirrel said in a mad rush.

She smiled at him. "You too, Fare."

CHAPTER THREE

There was such a strange, mixed vibe in the dining hall when Paris entered that she didn't know whether to be excited or nervous about it. Several new faces gave her tentative glances when she strode over to the buffet line.

There are new students. She picked up a warm plate from the end of the long table along the back wall.

There hadn't been a new student at Happily Ever After College since Paris. And she was the first one in a while. Enrollment had been down, which was one reason that Uncle John had been able to get Paris into the college. Well, and also because it was a protected place that could keep her safe from the Deathly Shadow. She didn't know any of that at the time or that Papa Creola and Mama Jamba were orchestrating such things.

Several women in their blue gowns, sans the pink ribbons around the collar, pointed at Paris.

Apparently, they haven't learned that pointing is rude. Paris loaded up her plate with biscuits and some of Chef Ash's specialty butter like sage and dill and garlic and herb. It was a carb load kind of day.

Paris knew that she stood out in her black leather jacket and combat boots, but she would have even if she wore the fairy godmother uniform because she was different. She wasn't a plain fairy. She was the only half-fairy, half-magician alive, and it made her look and feel different from others, according to many. Also, her demon blood put a mysterious glint in her eyes.

However, as Paris glanced around the room of new students, she got the impression that many of them were different too.

"They aren't all fairies," Christine said at Paris' side. She'd approached from behind and seemed to read her mind.

"Headmistress Starr opened enrollment to other races?" Paris asked in sudden disbelief, realizing that's why the newbies appeared different. There were magicians and elves, which had subtle physical appearance differences.

For magicians, it was mostly in their demeanor since most fairies had their wings glamoured not to appear. Fairies were also prettier and usually more shapely, whereas magicians were plainer and often wore a speculative look. Fairies mostly wore careful smiles. Well, the ones at Happily Ever After College anyway.

Elves were much easier to discern because of their pointy ears and willowy look.

"Yeah, I bet most of them don't pass the entrance exam." Christine picked up a piece of bacon from the heated tray and took a bite. "Headmistress Starr is trying something new in a hope to boost enrollment, but let's admit it, magicians don't have a romantic bone in their body."

"I resent that statement as a magician." Paris lowered her chin and regarded her friend with hooded eyes.

"Cool. Go ahead, tell me who sang *I Will Always Love You*," Christine ordered, still chewing.

Paris snapped her fingers, the name on the tip of her tongue. "That one lady, with the hair and the face. You know, the one."

Christine smiled victoriously. "I do, but you don't. You're the one person of a small minority who can't easily supply the name Whitney Houston to that question."

Paris scoffed. "Like I'm going to know the name of some singer from the mortal world. That doesn't prove anything."

"Fine, in what movie did Tom Cruise's character say, 'You complete me'?" Christine asked.

"Can we stop playing this ridiculous game that's robbing me of the will to live?" Paris turned and made her way over to her usual spot at the dining table next to Hemingway, Chef Ash, and Penny. Thankfully the newbie students hadn't taken over her and Christine's spots.

"I think what you meant to say is, 'I don't know the answer to that question even though the rest of the world does,'" Christine sang beside her.

"Nobody knows that, and it again proves nothing." Paris slid into her seat, smiling briefly at Hemingway on her left.

"Hey, guys," Christine said to the group. "I'm sure none of you will know this, but shout it out if you do. In what movie did Tom Cruise's character say, 'You complete—"

"Jerry Maguire," Chef Ash and Penny nearly yelled in unison before she finished the question.

Christine shrugged and glanced mischievously at Paris. "Look at those nobodies."

Paris rolled her eyes. "Fine, I'm not romantic. That's no news flash to anyone."

"It's because you're a magician," Christine stated matter-of-factly.

"Magicians can be romantic," Hemingway argued.

"We shall see." Christine pointed around the room, indicating the new students. "We'll also see how elves do as fairy godmothers creating matches since they're mostly concerned with their chakras and finding personal enlightenment over romance."

"I think a little diversity in the fairy godmothers will go a long way," Chef Ash offered.

"Yeah, look at the unique solutions Paris has brought to us because she approaches things differently as a halfling," Penny added.

"Sass," Christine said plainly, sticking the rest of the bacon she'd been working on into her mouth. "She brings a lot of sass."

"Christina, you're one to talk," Paris teased. "Are you sure you're a fairy? You have a lot of attitude for one."

Everyone around the table laughed.

"That's definitely true," Christine said proudly. She reached over and stole a piece of bacon off Chef Ash's plate, their eyes meeting briefly.

"You know there's a whole pile of bacon up there where I put it, right?" Chef Ash pointed at the buffet line.

Christine took another bite, an unapologetic glint in her eyes. "But it's so far away."

"But you're lazy like fairies, so maybe you are one," Paris joked.

Again the group laughed. This time, from a few people down the table, Becky Montgomery looked over, a seething expression in her eyes, her chin low and hostility written in her piercing expression.

"Hey now," Chef Ash said through a chuckle. "We're not lazy."

"You're not," Paris stated. "But most fairies also don't like to sweat or get their hands dirty."

Christine grimaced with disgust. "Why in the world would we want to do that? We're not a bunch of giants and gnomes."

"Agreed," Chef Ash stated. "I don't know how you do it, Hemingway, working on the grounds every day."

His eyes slid to Paris' before he glanced across the table at his friend. "It's the love of nature that gets me out there."

"That makes sense," Chef Ash agreed. "A fairy thrives on love."

"And I take hot, elaborate bubble baths at the end of the day to get off all the dirt." Hemingway winked at Paris. She knew that he loved his work taking care of the Enchanted Grounds of Happily Ever After College, but he was also strong and hardworking, and that was due to his magician blood—although no one knew that.

The five friends laughed again, earning another look of contempt from Becky, who wasn't talking excitedly to her friends like usual. Around her, most were whispering, and many times their eyes flicked in her direction.

Paris knew that many were talking about Becky and her newly revealed family secret.

"Have you all heard that different races will be allowed to do more than enroll here at the college?" Penny whispered, leaning low over the table.

Paris' focus snapped to her friend. "Say what? Tell me more."

"Well, it's only a rumor," Penny began. "But it stands to reason that if Headmistress Starr is considering educating elves and magicians as godmothers, she's also considering bringing in experts to teach who aren't fairies."

"Really?" Chef Ash asked. "That's a neat idea. Capitalize on expert resources."

"Yeah," Penny continued. "Apparently when Bermuda Laurens, who knows the most about magical creatures was here, Headmistress Starr talked to her about teaching a special lecture on the subject as a guest speaker. She has to get approval from Saint Valentine and the board, but if they're allowing other races to enroll as students, it seems likely."

"I don't know," Christine said through a bite. "The students still have to pass their entrance exam so there are no free rides here. They have to prove themselves to stay, and like I was telling Paris, I bet most of them don't make it."

"I don't know why you have to be so cynical," Chef Ash argued. "Paris passed her exams."

"Paris is Paris," Christine said like this was a sufficient argument. "She's half-fairy, so even if she's an overthinking, unromantic magician, she still has a mushy part to her."

"Are you referring to my butt?" Paris pretended to be serious.

"Yes," Christine chirped before returning her attention to the others. "I'm totally open to all these new changes, but if I'm honest, I think that fairy godmothers are fairies for a reason.

"We're hardwired to promote love. We're all about emotions and creating butterfly feelings. It seems illogical to think that hippie elves and practical magicians will excel at something that's always been our job. You don't see me trying to get a job at the House of Fourteen solving the world's complex problems."

"But if you did," Paris began, "you'd bring a different perspective that would provide varied solutions."

"I think," Hemingway drew out the last word, "that the thing about multiple races is we employ different ways to approach things.

There's more than one way to create love, and Paris has helped the fairy godmothers consider new options. Fairies could solve complex world problems by bringing their devotion to love to negotiations or whatever it was."

"How about the elves?" Christine argued. "What do they bring?"

"Oh, they're useless," Hemingway joked. "They're going to sit around smoking their peace pipes and talking about their navels."

The group all laughed again.

This time Becky glared more forcefully in their direction before saying, "It's really rude to make fun of me when I'm right here."

Many around her and Paris' friends glanced in her direction, this time not trying to hide their curiosity.

"So, Psycho Pants," Christine sang, pushing her empty plate away. "We weren't talking and laughing about you. I know it's shocking that every conversation doesn't involve you and your family drama, but some of us don't care. So what that your family puts on a big show as the most elite fairy godmothers and has a scandalous tooth fairy black sheep hiding in your attic."

"My sister isn't hiding in the attic," Becky spat, loud enough that those around them not looking at her now were.

"No, Courtney Montgomery is at Loose Teeth College," Paris stated. "Strange that you have an identical twin and never cared to mention it."

"Even stranger," Hemingway mused, combing his hand over his chin speculatively, "is that Courtney and her friends figured out how to get onto Enchanted Grounds. I've been trying to figure out how, and the only thing that Headmistress Starr and I can decide is that they must've had insider information."

All eyes snapped onto Becky. Her eyes widened in horror. "I didn't tell Courtney anything!"

"No, you probably didn't do it knowingly," Penny said in a quiet voice, her eyes on the table as if she was working it out.

Chef Ash shrugged. "A little information here and there could go a long way, especially for fairies who are in the same bubble as us here."

"Which Loose Teeth College unfortunately is," Christine stated.

"I didn't tell Courtney and her friends how to get in here!" Becky exclaimed once again.

Christine gave her a "Bless your heart" look and nodded. "Of course you did. That's how they got into our grounds. I heard they destroyed the Serenity Gardens."

Hemingway nodded. "I can attest to that."

"And they attacked the observatory," Penny added.

Another nod from Hemingway. "Correct also."

"The grounds are locked up from them now, right?" Penny asked in a scared voice.

"We know to look for them," Hemingway consoled.

"So they could come back," Christine stated.

"Headmistress Starr is working on a way to resolve things," Paris said with confidence. "And Courtney's wand is broken so I don't think she'll try to break in here any time soon."

"Yeah, those evil tooth fairies use the dark magic from the Fang Wellspring." Christine shook her head. "A bunch of goth rejects who buy up all the black nail polish and keep Marilyn Manson concerts sold out."

Many around the table laughed. Not Becky. And not a new student who appeared to be a magician with a sour attitude.

Paris wasn't sure if it was Becky's hostile looks aimed in her direction, which were probably silently followed by many death threats in her head, but she got the distinct feeling of evil nearby. She remembered Faraday's warning to be on guard because the Montgomerys would be after her now for revenge.

Finding it hard to shake the feeling of evil somewhere close by her, Paris pulled her attention back in the direction of her friends. She'd have to stay vigilant because something told her that the threats from Loose Teeth College and the Montgomerys weren't gone.

CHAPTER FOUR

"Today might be your most important day at Happily Ever After College," Headmistress Willow Starr began, poised at the front of the classroom, her hands pressed calmly in front of her.

"To think I almost played hooky today and skipped this class," Christine muttered from the corner of her mouth in Paris' direction.

She stifled a laugh and kept her focus on the headmistress, standing tall in her blue gown with the pink sash tied into a pretty bow around her neck—the mark of a graduate fairy godmother.

"Today, you're going to pick out what your graduation project will be," Willow continued, creating an excited stir around the room. "The success of this project will decide not only whether you pass and become a fairy godmother, but FGA also uses it for placement purposes. Saint Valentine and his agents review these projects and assign graduates accordingly. The most successful students have gone on to work on high-level cases that have huge ramifications on love."

"Penny, doesn't your mom work on the lowest level cases, doing things that really don't affect love?" Becky asked from behind Paris. "That's why you're so poor, right? Because your mom is the worst fairy godmother."

She tensed, wondering why the fairy wanted her wrath so badly.

Becky could as easily be quiet and not bully when there was so much ammunition aimed at her, but she didn't seem to know what was good for her. Paris turned in her seat and glared at her nemesis.

"I believe the worst fairy godmother would be the one who raises a fairy who sabotages our college," Paris retorted. "Just think how much the Knees have brought the love meter down with their crimes and hateful ways."

Becky returned the murderous glare. "It's not Mother's fault that Courtney turned out bad. Everyone knows that twins are always born opposite with a good and an evil one."

"Which one are you?" Paris pretended there was a choice.

"For a first, there were two bad ones born together," Christine joked. "Evil and eviler."

"I'm the good twin!" Becky exclaimed.

Paris nodded, giving her a mock look of approval. "Sure, you are… whatever you have to tell yourself."

"Good and evil is a scale, anyway," Christine stated. "For the Montgomerys, I think it's skewed more toward the wicked side."

"I got into Happily Ever After College," Becky argued. "I can't be evil."

"Right," Paris drew out the word. "Because Agent Ruby wasn't evil or anything. I think we've had sufficient evidence that it's all relative."

"It's not like your mother wouldn't have pulled strings to get you into the college if you didn't qualify," Christine added. "But man, Courtney must be awful if even Virginia Montgomery couldn't get her into Happily Ever After College."

"All cases are important at FGA because they promote love," Willow cut in, trying to recapture the students' attention. "It's simply that some involve more complex investigations and solutions."

Paris turned back in her seat, offering Becky one last scowl. "So Saint Valentine reviews these papers we write?"

The headmistress smiled politely at her. "Your final project is a bit more involved than writing a paper."

"Yeah, this isn't elementary school, but since you probably didn't go to school, you wouldn't know that," Becky jabbed from behind Paris.

This time, Paris showed great restraint and didn't turn. Instead, she glanced at Christine beside her and said, "Some of us still act like we're in elementary school."

The truth was, Paris didn't know much about elementary school or any formal schools since Uncle John homeschooled her. That mostly consisted of helping him with detective cases and watching a lot of television, but she didn't feel shortchanged in the least.

Willow cleared her throat, again trying to steer the conversation back on topic. "As I was saying, the final project is quite involved. The idea is to use many of the concepts you've learned here at Happily Ever After College to create a business that promotes love somehow.

"Many fairy godmothers have side businesses because they help to facilitate their cases and make matches. Also, it provides an extra income. Mae Ling, for instance, had a very successful nail salon before she came to Happily Ever After College to take the head professor position."

Paris was suddenly very overwhelmed by the idea of creating her own business. She'd thought the final project would involve writing a thesis or crafting a mega dessert. She already had to wear a dress and dance in front of everyone at the college and their families for graduation. Now she had to create a viable business. She didn't know where to start.

"I'm going to create a florist shop," a student at the back of the classroom offered.

Willow nodded with approval. "Yes, that would be a good one as flowers promote love and many men give them as a way of showing their affection."

"How about a chocolate shop?" Penny asked.

The headmistress beamed. "That's a lovely idea. Chocolate is a natural aphrodisiac and elevates good moods."

"I'm going to start a fashion consulting business," Christine stated. "That way, I can stop people from wearing denim shirts or jean jackets with jeans. No one needs to wear a Canadian tuxedo."

Paris laughed. "Is that what that's called?"

"Yes," Christine answered. "I'll also stop people from wearing red and green together. You're not a Christmas tree, people. And it's August. Just don't."

Willow offered a small chuckle, amused by Christine's regular antics. "I think that by helping others to feel more confident about their dress, you can promote love indirectly." She looked around the classroom. "This gives you all an idea of different businesses that you can start. To help you with initial costs, the school gives you all five thousand dollars."

This brought many excited whispers from around the room.

"That's more money than Penny has seen in her entire life," Becky teased.

Unfortunately, many of the students found this funny and laughed.

"It's way less than your mom paid to get you into Happily Ever After College," Paris remarked, not turning around.

Willow waited until the noise settled down, ignoring the exchange of insults. "For many of you, that amount of money will be more than enough to cover start-up costs. However, if you need additional funds, you'll have to get creative and try to get donations or negotiate trades."

"Or ask Mommy to give you the money," Christine stated, her comment intended for Becky.

"The business doesn't have to turn a profit," Willow continued, "that's not the project's intent. It's simply to show a measurable impact on the love meter. During testing, we'll use individual love meters to assess each of the businesses. The amount of love produced will therefore be a factor when Saint Valentine makes assignments."

"What score does one have to get to be assigned as an agent at FGA?" Paris asked.

This produced many gasps around the room. Becky laughed rudely. Willow, however, offered a caring look.

"Paris, women aren't assigned as agents at FGA," she explained. "That role has always been given to males to create a balance. Males assess cases and assign and supervise them. Fairy godmothers are always females."

The only reply to this was simple to Paris. "Why?"

This caused more whispers around her.

"Well, as I said, it's about balance," Willow answered.

"Wouldn't a balance be men and women in the same roles?" Paris argued. "That way we could bring our unique skills to the positions."

"We're called fairy godmothers," Becky said in an annoyed tone. "Fairy godfathers don't match Cinderellas and Prince Charmings."

"Why not?" Paris countered. "Men are equally as capable of creating matches as women. Maybe they're better in different ways. Why can't women assess and analyze cases and supervise?"

The headmistress looked dumbfounded by these questions. "Because that's not the way we do it."

"Where are agents trained?" Paris asked. "Is there a college for them?"

"Well, no," Willow answered. "Saint Valentine appoints them. Because they aren't in the field creating matches, they don't need education the same way we do. They serve more as managers."

"How can they manage if they aren't educated about what we do?" Paris questioned.

"You seriously misunderstand how things work," Becky criticized. "Women are the naturally romantic gender and the right choice for matching a Cinderella and Prince Charming."

"I think that's completely unfounded," Paris stated with confidence. "This is like the notion that we should solely focus our attention as fairy godmothers matching royalty and famous people."

Becky sighed. "Of course we should. When a prince matches with an eligible princess, it promotes love all around the world because their love inspires people."

Paris rolled her eyes. "Until the masses find out that it's a complete sham of a marriage because Prince Whatever doesn't love Princess Fakery and is in love with his maid or the girl who lived in a distant land or was the heir to a competing nation."

Becky scoffed, obviously offended. "Princes don't marry their maids. We would never arrange a marriage like that."

"So you do admit that we arrange those marriages?" Paris questioned. "That's not our job as fairy godmothers. It's to bring two people together who are totally and madly in love with each other. Not only that, but our ultimate goal is to create love.

"That's not simply about pairing up two people. That's about healing families. Helping children and parents to get along. Making friends. Why are we confining ourselves to only romantic love when love of all types impacts the love meter?"

Willow's mouth fell open and shut several times before she finally recovered. "You bring up some excellent points. I have to admit that I don't have the answers to these questions. I do think that Saint Valentine might. I'd be happy to set up a meeting with him for you."

"That's ridiculous!" Becky exclaimed. "She can't meet with Saint Valentine to ask such questions. He'll be downright offended."

"I don't think so," Willow argued. "The current Saint Valentine enjoys hearing new ideas and is trying to challenge old ways of thinking. This is the type of thing he'd be interested in."

"That's exactly why he's not going to stay in office long." Threat laced Becky's voice.

Paris sorely hoped she was wrong, but she knew that the former Agent Ruby wasn't the only one against the current Saint Valentine. His openness to progressive new ways was what made him unpopular with the old families like the Montgomerys.

Willow clapped her hands softly together. "Well, this has been a very stimulating conversation. I hope it's helped you all to start thinking of ideas for your businesses. You'll have from now until the end of the school year to launch the business so I encourage you to get right to work."

Paris sat back in her seat, a sudden idea occurring to her for a business. The conversation about creating love for all had sparked it. She wanted to bring people together of all sorts—couples, families, and friends. There was a surefire way to do that, which she thought would appeal to people of all kinds. However, for her business to work, she needed a lot more than five thousand dollars.

It appeared she'd have to pull on her resources. Thankfully she was connected to many powerful people—like Mother Nature and Father Time.

CHAPTER FIVE

"Paris, will you please stay behind?" Headmistress Willow Starr asked when she dismissed the class, and many students filed for the exit.

Now she was going to get it for challenging the old fairy godmother ways. Paris hung back, waiting for the other students to clear out. However, that didn't sound like the headmistress. Plus, Willow had offered to set up a meeting with Saint Valentine for Paris. So she figured she was paranoid.

"I think Mae Ling was right about you," Willow said when the last of the students had left the classroom.

Paris tensed, not sure what that statement meant.

Sensing her stress, Willow offered a thoughtful smile. "She said that she thought you'd bring much-needed change to the fairy godmothers. It seems the prophecy that Agent Ruby discovered about you might come to pass."

This did little to dispel the tension building in Paris' chest. When she went to the Great Library to investigate the prophecy, Paris learned that for it to come to pass, she had to graduate from Happily Ever After College, fall in love, and have her heart broken. Two of those three things seemed scary. One of them, she hoped was inevitable.

"It's progressive thinking like yours that I think the fairy godmothers need to evolve into the modern world and continue to bring love to more people," Willow continued.

"Well, I hope I didn't say anything too challenging in front of the class," Paris commented.

The fairy godmother shook her head. "You said a lot that I hadn't considered. I would like to set up a meeting with Saint Valentine and you."

"Is that why you asked me to stay behind?"

Headmistress Starr shook her head. "That can wait. You should focus on your final project. It will take a lot more of your time than you might think."

Paris gulped, having that exact thought. She didn't know how to budget expenses for herself. She didn't know how she was going to manage this huge business venture she wanted to create. However, Paris knew one thing with certainty—she wanted this business.

Before entering the class that morning, she had no idea that she wanted this so badly. Now, she couldn't consider not wanting it, not doing everything possible to make it happen. Something in her soul told her that the business was right. Plus, if things did fall through with this fairy godmother business, well, she'd have the business, and it would hopefully sustain her.

"I wanted to ask for your help getting to Loose Teeth College," Willow explained. "Although the tooth fairies have been quiet, I don't think that will last for long. You might've deterred Courtney from attacking anymore, but now that her family secret is out and as you said, her trust fund cut off, she's going to be angry and seeking revenge. The longer things stay quiet, the more worried I get that they're up to something big, plotting to harm Happily Ever After College."

"I can take you to the vortex. Are you going to try meeting with Headmistress Sham to come to a truce?"

Willow looked uncertain. "I'm going to try. I fear that it will be a long road to recovery. This feud has been going on for a long time, and I have valid reasons for not wanting to be associated with their college, which has always given Headmistress Sham a sour taste toward us."

"You want the attacks to end. So it should be as easy as leave us alone, and we'll leave you alone…as we were doing."

Headmistress Willow tipped her head back and forth. "I wish it were that easy, but Headmistress Sham wants more. Her students attacking us is a direct result of the lack of privileges that the tooth fairies have due to our fallout. At Happily Ever After College, we have the support of FGA and Saint Valentine that keeps us running successfully with many resources. Conversely, Loose Teeth College is very poor. The only thing they have supporting them is the Fang Wellspring."

"So this is about money?" Paris asked.

Willow nodded. "It usually is. Before we fell out completely, the Seelie queen, Helena MacGillie, was sending subsidies to Loose Teeth College to fund much of their ventures. However, when we severed the ties and refused to make amends, the queen cut all money to the tooth fairies."

"Well, then it sounds that Headmistress Sham will be all too happy to fix relations," Paris reasoned. "Then she can get her money again, and we'll be safe. It's a win-win."

"Again, I wish it were that simple. It was I who initially parted ways from Loose Teeth College, asking that they not associate with us any longer."

Paris blinked at the fairy godmother, shocked that the sweet woman had been so rude and alienating. "Why?"

"Well, because I don't approve of what they do. They create dark magic that many pull from. I had trouble condoning it for the longest time and finally had to make a choice. Associating with the tooth fairies had negative effects on Happily Ever After College. So our location was moved and hidden using the Bewilder Forest. Then Queen MacGillie found out, and because we must do things to her liking, she cut Loose Teeth College's funds, stating that unless there was harmony between us, she wouldn't support either of us."

"Since then, she's disallowed either tooth fairies or fairy godmothers from entering the Seelie court," Paris added, having heard this part of the history.

"That's correct," Willow affirmed. "What I want is for them to leave us alone, but I suspect that Headmistress Sham will want more than that. It's overdue, and we must put aside some of our differences and try to work things out. However, I do believe that will take a lot more than simply having a conversation after all this time."

"Well, I'm happy to show you where the vortex door is." Then Paris remembered. "But Faraday and I crashed the hot air balloon, and it's quite far away, over many lands that my halfling and demon blood created."

"Yes, so we'll need new transportation."

"I asked King Rudolf for another hot air balloon, but he didn't have any more."

"Do you think maybe your aunt can help us out?" Willow referred to Sophia and her dragon.

"I can ask. She was busy on a mission before, but that might've wrapped up by now."

"Thank you. I would greatly appreciate it. I want to stop any new attacks before things get out of hand. As vigilant as we are here at Happily Ever After College right now, I think the only way to be confident that we're safe is to go straight to the source."

"Okay, I'll message my aunt and let you know when I hear back." Paris moved for the door, not wanting to be late for her next class.

"Thank you," Willow called as she retreated. "Oh, and Paris…"

She paused at the door and gave the headmistress a questioning look. "Yes?"

"I'm looking forward to seeing your final project. I have a feeling it will be unlike anything we've seen before."

CHAPTER SIX

"I think it's burning my skin," Paris hissed, sucking in a sudden breath.

Christine sighed, shaking her head. "It's satin material. It's not hurting you."

"You don't know that. I'm allergic to soft materials such as this." Paris peered down, watching as the tailor, Juergen, pinned up the hem of the giant blue ball gown she was wearing. Paris had avoided it long enough and had to do the final fitting for the dress she'd wear for her ballroom dance at her graduation ceremony. Of course, that graduation wasn't guaranteed and hinged on the final project and whether she created a business that promoted love. Everything was coming to a head, and the pressure was mounting.

If Paris didn't pass, she could continue her education at Happily Ever After College. Many students took years to master the curriculum. It was only recently that Headmistress Starr and Mae Ling had said they thought she'd be ready for early graduation based on her exam scores. That meant Paris would be graduating with her friends —Christine and Penny.

"Satan," Christine chirped, tilting her head and squinting at the dress. "You're allergic to Satan, but satin and silk are fine. I dare say, the material makes you look like a princess."

Paris pretended to gag. "I thought you were my friend. Why would you say such a mean thing?"

Christine laughed, making some students practicing ballroom dancing with Wilfred look over momentarily. "You know, most think that being a princess is a good thing. It makes you royalty. And princesses are always pretty in their ball gowns."

Juergen got up to retrieve some more pins for the hem. Paris took this opportunity to sway her hips, trying to move in the dress. "I guess, but I don't need any prince saving me. I can't throw a roundhouse kick in this, but I think I could still kick butt if I needed to."

"Your final dance at graduation won't require any kicks of any sort," Wilfred said, striding over and evaluating Paris' dress.

"If I manage to find my feet, can I get extra points for throwing a kick?" Paris teased.

"Since I'll probably be your partner, I'd prefer that you didn't," the magitech AI butler stated.

"I think the train in the back should be longer, don't you?" Christine asked Wilfred, both of them inspecting her dress.

"I can hardly move in this thing," Paris complained. "How about we go with shorter and something in black leather?"

"No and no," Wilfred stated matter-of-factly.

Paris sighed, blowing her hair off her face.

"You'll hold up the train in one hand," Christine stated.

"Oh, great. I'm already worried about doing this final dance right and not falling on my face. Now I have to hold the train up and dance?"

"That's why practice will be key," Wilfred offered. "Again, you'll be dancing with me, and I'll lead you."

Paris nodded. "I'm glad I'm not dancing with a horse."

Wilfred blinked at her in confusion. "A horse? Why would you?"

"Is it because of your demon blood and horses loathe you?" Christine asked, seriously.

"No, it's because horses have two left feet." Paris laughed loudly at her joke.

A smile cracked on Christine's face. However, Wilfred didn't look amused.

"Oh, come on, Wil," Paris urged. "What do I have to do to get a laugh out of you?"

"I'm capable of many things, but laughing isn't one of them," the butler stated.

"Yeah, give our dance instructor a break. He already has to teach you to dance and shouldn't have to put up with your bad jokes too," Christine said.

"Incidentally," Paris began, holding back a grin. "Do you know how many dance teachers it takes to change a light bulb?"

"How many?" Christine indulged her.

"Five, six, seven, eight." Paris laughed.

Thankfully her friend laughed too, but again not Wilfred.

"Why are dance instructors changing light bulbs?" Wilfred asked, quite seriously. "Shouldn't that be someone else's job?"

Paris threw her hands up and rolled her eyes. "Oh, this is hopeless. I'll never get you to laugh."

He nodded. "I think the sooner you recognize that, the better. It's not a good use of your time and energy with your final project and end-of-year events approaching."

"You know that humor decreases stress and is good for you, right?" Paris countered.

"Wilfred is made of magitech and sits on a charging station in the basement at night," Christine argued with a laugh.

Paris stood still as Juergen returned to continuing pinning up the hem and altering her dress. "Well, it's good for me, and without my comedic nature, I'd be a bundle of nerves."

"Imagine if your jokes were good," Christine teased.

"Then imagine if my friends weren't total jerks," Paris joked, sending a mock scowl at the fairy.

"Wil," Christine began, walking around Paris and studying her dress. "Do you think the neckline should be lower?"

"I do," he answered.

"I don't," Paris argued.

"How about the sleeves, off the shoulder?" Christine continued, ignoring Paris.

Wilfred nodded. "That would be very elegant in that material."

"Is the material made of lava?" Paris joked. "My skin is on fire."

Arriving right in front of her again, Christine grinned. "You're not allergic to it. Whether you like it or not, you look beautiful in this already. You're going to be the belle of the ball during graduation."

Paris sighed. "Fine, I'll wear the dress, but I'm not wearing high heels."

"What else would you wear?" Wilfred asked, surprised.

She smiled wide, pulling up the dress to reveal her black combat boots. "These, of course."

CHAPTER SEVEN

Paris was distracted when she entered the dining hall for lunch, her attention on her phone as she messaged her Aunt Sophia. It didn't take long for the other woman to return her message, saying that she and Lunis would be happy to transport her and Willow to the vortex door the next day. The blue dragon could super-size himself for the excursion, ensuring there was more than enough room for all three of them.

The last message from her Aunt Sophia made Paris feel much better about her business idea for the final project. Sophia had said that it was brilliant, and she thought Mama Jamba would be happy to help, as well as some other experts. That meant Paris needed to enlist the help of a few others. Hopefully, she'd create a business that promoted lots of love for people of all types.

Because she was distracted, Paris ran straight into a new student. More accurately, it wasn't like the woman had accidentally run into her because she was juggling carrying her hot potato soup and freezing ice water. It was like she'd run right for Paris instead.

Hot soup slammed into Paris' chest, burning her instantly and covering her front. Then she was immediately doused with ice water, which she was thankful for. Paris jumped back as everyone around her gasped from the collision.

However, Paris went straight into action, pointing at her front and magically cleaning the liquids from her. They disappeared instantly, and thankfully she didn't feel the heat of the burn, although her skin on the upper portion of her chest was red with irritation.

The newbie student who'd run into Paris didn't look like most of the fairies in Happily Ever After College. She was wearing the blue gown uniform, so her true hair color was unknown—having taken on the familiar bluish-gray tone as everyone else's.

Her thick hair was straight as a board and cut in a flat line above her shoulders. In her brown eyes, there was a strange glint of mischief that was rare to see on someone's face at Happily Ever After College. Most striking was that she was undoubtedly a magician based on the energy that Paris was reading from her. There was something about magicians that registered differently than fairies.

Paris ignored the many concerned gasps around her, checking to ensure she'd cleaned herself up enough and her skin wasn't too affected by the hot potato soup. She expected the new student to apologize or ask if she was okay.

What she didn't expect was for the woman to put her hands on her hips and say, "Well, now I have to get more soup."

Paris blinked at her as if she misunderstood what she said. "Are you serious?"

Before Rude McRudeson could reply, Hemingway was at her side, looking her over. "Are you okay? Was that potato soup? It can really scald."

Paris nodded, keeping her eye on the new student who was running her curious gaze over Hemingway suddenly. "Yeah, I'm fine. Thankfully, the new student quickly doused me with ice water right after throwing hot soup on me."

"Yeah, and now I have to get a new drink too," the woman complained.

"We have an abundance." Hemingway ran his gaze over the new student, his eyes disapproving. "I believe an apology would be nice."

"I agree," the student said. "I did lose my lunch and have to go stand back in that line." The magician pointed at the buffet line, which wasn't moving since most were watching Paris after the collision.

"I meant that it would be nice to apologize for throwing hot soup all over Paris," Hemingway stated. "If she hadn't been so quick-thinking with her magic, she could have been severely burned."

"Well, and I also should be thanked for thinking of throwing my ice water on her," the student said. "That's why she didn't get burned."

Paris tilted her head, studying the magician. "It's funny because it seemed like you also threw the soup straight on me too."

"I noticed that too," Hemingway said skeptically.

"You ran into me," the newbie said.

"What's your name?" Hemingway narrowed his eyes at the woman.

"Zora Tali," the woman stated. "You're Hemingway, right? I have you for my next class."

"Can't wait," Hemingway said dryly.

"Me too." Zora batted her fake eyelashes at him.

Paris wanted to slap the woman with butterfly-like wings attached to her eyes across the face. There was something off about her, but she knew that Headmistress Starr was trying to open up enrollment to allow more diversity. Also, the new generations weren't as interested in becoming fairy godmothers anymore because their traditional look was so old and their ways engrained in outdated practices.

Hopefully, that would change. Opening up enrollment to other races was something Paris supported unless it meant that a bunch of evil magicians would be joining their ranks. The one thing that made her feel marginally better was that the new students had to pass the entrance exams at the end of the day. Otherwise, today was their first and last day at Happily Ever After College. She secretly hoped that Zora Tali didn't score well on her tests.

"I can't wait to hear that apology for dumping hot soup all over Paris," Hemingway stated in an annoyed voice.

"Well, don't hold your breath." Zora strode back toward the buffet line. "I'm the one who has to stand in this long line once again, but at least so does precious Paris."

"Actually," Hemingway grabbed Paris by the hand and tugged her forward. "I'm certain that Chef Ash will serve you right at the front. He knows what you like and probably has it ready. Let's go."

Paris allowed herself to be hauled to the front of the line and didn't hide her smirk as she glanced over her shoulder at Zora, who was shooting her a murderous glare.

Something wasn't right about that magician. Hopefully, she'd be gone by the end of the day, but if not, Paris would keep an eye on her.

CHAPTER EIGHT

"As a fairy, I'm not prone to violence," Christina said when Paris and Hemingway sat at the dining table. "But I think I'm going to put that girl in a headlock." She nodded in the magician's direction. Zora looked really put out at having to stand in the long buffet line again.

Thankfully, Chef Ash had seen the incident and went and collected a plate of food for Paris. He promised to join them at the table once he'd taken the soup off the buffet. It was the first time he'd ever served it and had said it was a special request from Zora, the new student. However, since she appeared to be firing it at students like a weapon, Chef Ash didn't like the idea of keeping it for another incident.

"She's a real pill," Hemingway agreed. "I don't understand how she got in through the initial assessment."

"Well, Paris passed that too," Christine joked. "So apparently anyone can get a chance."

"But you have to prove yourself to stay," Penny added.

"Hey, not just anyone can get in here," Paris argued.

"That's true," Hemingway consoled. "Usually, there's an application and an essay students have to submit."

Christine leaned in Paris' direction. "Tell me about the subject of the essay you wrote to get into Happily Ever After College. Was it like mine and a full analysis of Ross and Rachel's complete love affair from *Friends*? Or did you take the more traditional approach and do a synopsis of the movie, *The Notebook*?"

Paris laughed. "You know I didn't write an essay, weirdo."

"Oh, that's right," Christine sang. "You have hookups who got you into the college."

"But I didn't pay my way to get in here," Paris argued. "Uncle John was trying to keep me safe and out of jail."

"Which makes you about as bad as the new riffraff that's infected this place." Becky leaned over to join the conversation, although no one had invited her.

However, this was something that she and Paris could finally agree on. Zora Tali was riffraff and didn't give off pleasant vibes as she butted into conversations in the buffet line and looked around the dining hall with narrowed eyes.

"Paris has manners," Hemingway argued. "She was only ever in trouble for trying to help others. Something you might want to consider."

"I have manners," Becky stated as if this had been the part of his point they'd been arguing about. "The new student is a magician, which I think proves that we shouldn't consider bad seeds like that race as godmothers. They don't belong here." She gave Paris a pointed look that seemed to say, "Hint, hint. That means you, as well."

Paris rolled her eyes and turned her attention away from Becky, who was only looking to get a rise out of her. Chef Ash made his way to the dining table then, and she smiled at him.

"Thanks for having a plate ready for me." She indicated the food in front of her.

He smiled at her. "I was happy to. I'm sorry that witch over there threw soup on you. It looked quite deliberate."

Paris glanced at Zora Tali, who had her head huddled with some other students. "I'm glad I'm not paranoid. I thought I imagined that."

Christine shook her head. "Oh, no. I saw her make a beeline for you as soon as you entered the dining hall. What did you do to that student?"

Paris shrugged. "I've never met her before. Maybe my mom put her criminal family in jail, or my dad hunted down her demon father. She might be mad at me by association."

"She's definitely a bad seed," Chef Ash said in a low voice. "While I was serving food, I heard her recruiting students to play a game with her. Except chanting Bloody Mary in a dark bathroom is no game. I told the students to dismiss the idea right away and that we'd be conjuring no harmful spirits."

"What?" Paris asked. "I know you said Blood Mary is a real thing. What are we, teenagers at a slumber party? Why would Zora try to do such a thing?"

"It's a thing," Penny stated. "If a group is successful, the spirit they summon can be quite dangerous."

Paris glanced at Hemingway, knowing that he knew all too well how dangerous a haunting could be. The spirit of his dead mother had destroyed the Bewilder Forest.

"I don't think any of our students will be daft enough to do it with Zora," Chef Ash continued. "Also, I have high hopes that she'll be gone before the end of the day. So I'm sure it won't be a concern."

Paris nodded, but something in the pit of her stomach told her not to be so sure. Zora had already proven to be menacing. Now she was trying to get students to conjure an evil spirit. If she did somehow pass her entrance exams, Paris would stop her antics before they went too far.

Unfortunately, babysitting a newbie student would be difficult since she needed to help Headmistress Starr get to Loose Teeth College and start a business that promoted love. However, there was nothing more important than protecting Happily Ever After College.

CHAPTER NINE

From the back of the greenhouse, Paris kept her eyes on Zora Tali. The magician was hard at work, seeming to make friends with multiple students. Paris didn't buy that though. There was a disingenuous quality in her eyes.

"You know that dirt goes in the pot, not on the table, right?" Hemingway asked beside her workstation.

Paris glanced down and realized she'd dumped a mound of potting soil on the table next to her pot—not having been paying attention as she watched Zora across the greenhouse. They were repotting light bulbs, which were plant bulbs, but when they sprouted and bloomed, they made a bright spot of light from their center. They were similar to the twinkling flowers that had been in the Bewilder Forest before its destruction.

Hemingway hoped to plant the light bulbs along the path he'd been working on in the new forest. It didn't have any lights for at night, not that anyone would dare to go in there at night yet, not with a gargoyle and who knew what else on the loose.

Hemingway and Bermuda Laurens had ventured into the new Bewilder Forest a few times without Paris. Thankfully, they could navigate their way through there without getting lost or tricked, now that they'd started to figure out the different riddles created by her fairy, magician, and demon parts.

However, it wasn't safe for anyone else to attempt it, and most of their field trips had turned into unexpected adventures. Once most of the forest was mapped and understood and infrastructure put into place, like walking paths and light bulbs for at night, Headmistress Starr said she'd consider allowing students and other staff into the forest.

Paris was nervous and excited to show the fairy godmother the Bewilder Forest and different parts of the terrain created by her blood when they ventured over it to the vortex door. That would be a good opportunity for the headmistress to get a scope of the land and understand how best to protect those who explored it.

"Yeah, I guess I'm a bit distracted," Paris admitted, scooping up the dirt and sticking it in the pot.

Hemingway followed her line of sight and nodded. "Yeah, that new student is giving magicians a bad name."

Paris offered him a smile. "I think her mischievous nature is more due to personality than the race she belongs to. Most magicians I know are amazing people."

He batted his eyes at her. "You mean your parents, right? And the rest of the Beaufont clan?"

"As well as you." She blushed.

"Why thank you."

"Hey, I wanted to ask for your help on creating my final project," Paris began in a low voice, not wanting anyone to overhear her. She was nervous about the elaborate business idea she had in mind and intimidated by the scope of it all.

He arched a curious eyebrow and gave her a look that said, "Go on. I'm listening and interested."

"So my idea is to create a farm-to-table restaurant," Paris explained. "I'd like it to be a full experience, so the place is on the farm where the vegetables, fruit, herbs, and dairy products are grown."

He beamed, his eyes suddenly filled with excitement. "So you'll have animals?"

She nodded. "This whole idea is so I can have goats."

They both laughed. "And you need my help with the crops, I'm guessing?"

"Yes, I know it will take a bit to get going, but there are fast-growing methods I've been practicing from the textbook."

Hemingway gave her a look of warning, but she paused him, holding up a hand.

"I know you've warned me against fast-growing methods before and how they can backfire," Paris stated. "However, I think with your help and supervision, I can pull it off."

"It's a stellar idea, and I can see how it will promote love."

"Thanks," Paris chirped. "My idea is that it brings love and happiness to all. I mean, a couple can go on a magical date there and fall in love over a candle-lit dinner. Also, a family can pick berries and have a nice picnic on the grounds, bonding them. Friends of all sorts can meet up to watch the animals play, then have drinks at the bar."

"I love that it's about bringing love to all types," Hemingway said, but with a reluctant tone.

"What is it?" Paris asked.

"Goats should be fine," he answered. "I'd warn you against having horses."

She laughed. "Yeah, don't worry. I'm staying as far from those beasts who loathe me because of my demon blood as possible. I'll have chickens, goats, sheep, and maybe a peacock."

He chuckled too. "Of course. You must have a peacock."

"And there will be orchards and vegetable patches of all types. Oh, and a vineyard and so much more."

"It sounds amazing." Again though, there was an edge of doubt in his voice.

"What is it?" she asked once more.

"Well, I love that you're going so big with your business," he began. "It's much more than any student has ventured to do in the past, creating not only a business but a business inside a business with a farm and all."

"You're worried about my budget," Paris guessed.

"Bingo," he answered.

"Well, I thought about that, and although my family is loaded, I don't want to cheat that way," Paris explained. "So I'm enlisting the help of my friends."

"Oh?" he asked curiously.

"Yeah, Aunt Sophia said that Mama Jamba will give me a fertile plot of land in the perfect location," she stated.

"Wow, you really do have the coolest friends."

"Yes, I do." Paris winked at him. "Aunt Sophia also said she has some friends who can help with tending to the grounds and the restaurant. Apparently, they've been looking for something new to do after being stuck at a castle in Scotland for a few centuries."

"You have really interesting friends too," he sang.

"Yes, I do," Paris repeated. "I hope that Chef Ash can help me with the menu, and if you're willing, maybe you'll help me with the initial planting."

"Of course," he stated at once, but once more, reluctance showed in his eyes.

"What is it?" Paris was starting to sound like a broken record, constantly repeating herself.

"Well," he drew out the word. "I'm happy to help, but my schedule might be getting a bit fuller."

"Oh? Is your teaching schedule getting busier with increased enrollment?"

"Yeah, and also, I took another job."

Paris didn't expect this reply. "Really? Where? Here at the college?"

He shook his head. "No. Remember Astrid from the Glowing Orchid?"

"Of course."

"Well, when I was hanging out on Roya Lane when the demons were at Happily Ever After College, I went into her shop a few times," he explained. "We got to talking, and she said she needed someone to go on different expeditions to find unique and rare magical plants around the world."

"Wow, are you serious? You're taking the job?"

Nervousness surfaced in his eyes when he nodded in confirmation.

"What about teaching?" Paris asked.

Hemingway shrugged. "I think it will take me away too much for me also to teach. You know I constantly have the stress about losing my job, so it's probably time I started something else."

Pairs gulped. She knew that if anyone revealed that he was a magician, he might get discharged by FGA and the board from teaching. However, things were changing. That morning, their group had discussed Willow considering hiring non-fairies for teaching positions. There was no guarantee, but enrollment opening up had been a big step. Who knew how long it would take for other races to be allowed to teach.

"I understand." Paris found it difficult to keep the disappointment out of her voice.

"Well, and you'll be graduating soon, at a record speed," Hemingway consoled. "So it's not like you'll miss seeing me."

"I will, though. But I'm happy for you. That sounds like a fun and exciting opportunity." Paris worked to inject enthusiasm into her voice. "You'll get to travel and see the world and also work with plants, which I know is your passion."

"It's not the only thing I'm passionate about," he remarked with a heated look in his eyes.

Paris' insides fluttered, and she felt a twinge she'd never felt before in her chest. She knew that the prophecy was right. She'd been falling for the guy in front of her since the beginning. However, if that part of the prophecy was correct, it meant she'd also have her heart broken. Hemingway not being in her life, after they'd been through so much together, would break it. Still, Paris wanted the best for him, and all he'd ever known was Happily Ever After College. He needed this.

"I guess this will be a nice way to find yourself," Paris said after a long moment where their gazes remained locked, and everyone in the greenhouse seemed to disappear.

"Maybe. Or it will be a way to get away from myself once you're gone," he stated.

There was so much regret in his eyes suddenly. Everything was shifting so much at the college with changes and graduation on the way. It was as if she was moving on before she moved on, and Hemingway was preparing for her departure.

"Well, as the other Hemingway said," Paris began as the line from *The Sun Also Rises* surfaced in her mind and felt so appropriate for the moment, "You can't get away from yourself by moving from one place to another."

He smiled. "Paris Beaufont, you never cease to surprise me. That line couldn't be more perfect, and you're right. I guess I can't run from my problems. But Astrid is giving me the opportunity, and I think I should take it soon. I'm overdue to explore the world. However, I'm happy to help you start the farm. It's going to be amazing, and after you graduate, it will be a viable business to keep you busy when you're not spreading love as a fairy godmother."

Paris nodded, hiding the look in her eyes by glancing down at the pot she'd been working with. Hemingway had been honest, confiding in her his career plans. She'd told him about her business. However, she wasn't ready to tell anyone her ultimate career ideas for after she graduated. Maybe that was because they'd only recently occurred to her. Or perhaps because she was still surprised by the idea. Most would be when they found out that after everything, Paris didn't really want to become a fairy godmother after all.

CHAPTER TEN

When Paris went to Magical Cooking, she was again surprised by the vibe in the test kitchens—like the dining hall. A group of students was huddled around one workstation, their heads together and Zora Tali at the center. They were whispering and glancing over their shoulders with conspiratorial looks when Paris passed them.

"Shush, shush," Zora ordered them when Paris paused to regard the group.

"What's going on?" Paris received rude glares that she didn't think she deserved. She was used to being the center of attention at the school based on her history, but usually, she didn't receive so many dirty looks.

"Nothing for you to be concerned about." Zora waved her away.

"Riiiight," Paris strode away to the front of the classroom, looking forward to when Zora failed her exam and had to leave Happily Ever After College. She did seem better suited for a place like Loose Teeth College. That idea suddenly needled something in her mind, but before she could pursue it further, Chef Ash took his place at the front of the classroom, capturing everyone's attention.

"Welcome old students and new ones to Magical Cooking," he

began. "Since today is your first day for some of you, I'm going to ask that you spend this session reading through our textbook to familiarize yourself with the curriculum. This will hopefully aid you in your exam tonight—ensuring that you pass it."

Or hopefully fail, Paris thought, glancing over her shoulder to where Zora wasn't paying the slightest bit of attention, whispering to the crowd of students around her.

"The rest of you will work on perfecting your signature dishes," Chef Ash continued. "These will need to be made for the graduation ceremony, where they will be a part of your final assessment. It is this grade, along with the review of your final projects and your ceremonial dance, that Saint Valentine will consider when he places you. Therefore, getting this dish exactly right and wowing the judges is important." He grinned wide. "Also, it's my favorite event since I get to be a taste tester as well. So get to cooking!"

There was a flurry of activity as the students went to work either reading or cooking. Or if they were Zora, they went straight to talking.

"Good, don't study and flunk out," Paris muttered to Christine, indicating over her shoulder the newbie student.

Her friend nodded. "No kidding. That little witch tried to trip Penny in the corridor earlier when she was carrying a boatload of books and couldn't see what was in front of her."

"I never thought we'd get a bully to rival Becky." Paris narrowed her eyes at Zora.

"I know," Christine said as Chef Ash headed over in their direction. "I knew if you were there, you would've made her pay. Remember when you were always throwing pies on bullies' heads?"

Overhearing their conversation, Chef Ash laughed. "Oh, I miss the days of you making bullies pay with pies to the head."

"Hey, I use what's available to me," Paris replied. "Maybe I'll change my signature dish to a pie."

"No!" Christine exclaimed at once. "You must make your famous cheeseball. It's the best thing ever."

Paris reeled back from her friend's sudden excitement. "Wow, I didn't know you were that in love with it."

"I totally am," Christine stated. "If it's cheesy and nutty, it's for me."

"Sounds like I might qualify then." Chef Ash winked at Christine.

Paris had never seen her friend wear that nervous expression before. Christine blushed, pushing her hair behind her ear. "It's the perfect combination."

Feeling like a third wheel, Paris opened her textbook on the hunt for new recipes for her business venture.

"Unfortunately, I'm not blessed like this halfling with already having perfected my signature dish," Christine sang after a moment. "I'm going to go work on mine. Or maybe I can change my name to Guinevere Paris Beaufont, and everything will magically come naturally to me."

"Then you can be born with a host of enemies too," Paris offered. "Oh, and you can have a strange first name you didn't know was yours, a middle name that's totally hippish, and a last name that most can't pronounce."

Christine sighed dramatically. "That sounds fantastic. That's much cooler than the story of my birth when I got a recycled name."

"Say what?" Chef Ash asked.

"My older sister's name was Christine, but then I was born, and my parents thought I looked more like Christine, so they renamed her Samantha."

"You're kidding, right?" Paris was shocked.

"I'm afraid not," Christine replied. "They told their five-year-old that she had to give up her name because the new baby needed it. She was old enough to remember it. Guess who hates me to this day?"

"It's not your fault that your parents took her name back," Chef Ash said sensitively.

"That's what I said," Christine stated. "My sister asked me when I was older if I'd give her back her original name and take hers. I was like, nope, I don't want a boy's name."

"Wow, that was real diplomatic of you, Christina," Paris joked.

The fairy shook her head and trotted for the refrigerator section to fetch supplies. "You know I love it when you call me by the wrong name."

"I know, Christy," Paris teased, laughing before turning her attention to Chef Ash. "I wanted to ask your help with something for my final project."

"I'm happy to help. What is it?"

Paris told Chef Ash her idea for creating a farm-to-table restaurant. "I want to use some magical ingredients Anyway, I hoped you could help me craft the menu for the café."

Delight shone in his bright eyes. He pulled out the pencil he always kept behind one ear and went to work sketching on a piece of parchment, listing different recipes immediately. "Of course! This is a fantastic idea. Although a bit ambitious, but I think doable by you."

"Thanks." Paris beamed, grateful to have his endorsement. "I like the idea of creating a dining experience and using the freshest possible ingredients."

"Working in a place like that would tempt me," Chef Ash stated, making Paris reflexively tense.

"Although I appreciate that, I think my aunt is recruiting me a head chef." Paris didn't like the idea that both Hemingway and Chef Ash were considering leaving the college. She needed some things to stay the same in her world—even if she would be leaving it.

"Okay, but I'll definitely help with designing the menu," Chef Ash said as Christine returned with an armful of ingredients and also wearing a sullen look.

"That evil magician is still working to recruit other students to do this Bloody Mary ritual." Christine glanced at Zora Tali.

Chef Ash sighed. "I think Casanova, the tattle cat, already informed Headmistress Starr about this. However, I'm not worried since I don't think she'll pass her exams tonight, so don't worry too much about it."

"I know you said Bloody Mary was real," Paris remarked. "I know hauntings can be dangerous. Why do you seem so worried about Zora succeeding before she flunks out of her exams, Christine?"

Chef Ash whispered, "I don't know of any recent incidents that involve conjuring her, but in the past, Bloody Mary has done horrible things. She doesn't only haunt, but can hurt those who summon her."

"I hear that she rips your soul in two," Christine stated.

Chef Ash nodded. "Also, many people went missing when they summoned her."

"Who would be crazy enough to conjure up this evil demon?" Paris asked.

"Well, usually young girls do it on a dare when they're together," Chef Ash explained. "However, there are some specifics on how you have to perform the ritual for it to work. Therefore, most of the time, thankfully, it doesn't work."

"Seems that Zora is a daredevil who likes drama," Christine stated.

"She's probably looking for ways to make friends," Chef Ash offered.

Christine laughed. "Yeah, then why is she throwing hot soup on people?"

"Well, Paris is the biggest name here at the college," Chef Ash answered. "Maybe she thought the display would give her a reputation right off the bat."

"It did," Christine stated.

"So who was Bloody Mary?" Paris asked. "Wasn't she a queen of England?"

"That's what some of the legends would have you believe," Chef Ash stated. "That's not the Bloody Mary the ritual supposedly conjures. It involves chanting in front of a dark mirror, and you need a certain number of people and artifacts to do it. For that reason, I highly doubt that Zora and her recruits will do it. However, the evil spirit that comes through the mirror is Mary Worth."

"Yeah," Christine said in an excited rush. "She was a witch who killed a bunch of girls during the Salem trials. They believed that she lured them from their homes, murdered them, and bathed in their blood."

Paris shivered with disgust. "That's horrible."

"It is," Chef Ash affirmed. "Allegedly, when the townspeople captured Mary Worth, she performed a curse before they executed her that anyone who spoke her name in front of a mirror would bring her back. According to legend, the blood of the girls she killed chained her to the Earth, making it possible for her to return in physical form if someone summoned her."

"But like Ash said," Christine began, "the ritual is a lot more complicated than chanting in front of a mirror. So thankfully, the records of her returning have been few."

"How do you get rid of her if someone successfully summons her?" Paris asked.

"That, I don't know," Chef Ash answered. "Unfortunately, most haven't survived her if they conjure her. Many go missing, mysteriously. Only a few have gotten away."

Christine nodded. "I think once the place where they summoned her is empty, that she doesn't have the anchor to stay in physical form and is pulled back into the mirror."

"So she either kills, takes people, or they get away," Paris remarked, her eyes distant and a foreboding feeling building in her stomach.

Chef Ash worked to force a light smile on his face. "Yeah, but don't worry. Soon Zora will be gone, and there won't be any Bloody Mary at Happily Ever After College."

Paris tried to copy his expression, but something deep down didn't feel right. She couldn't shake the feeling that something very sinister was on the horizon for the fairy godmothers.

CHAPTER ELEVEN

"Here I was having a nice day," Subner grumbled when Paris strode into the Fantastical Armory. "Now my good mood is surely gone."

"I'm sorry to ruin your usually sunny disposition with my existence," she muttered, watching as the greasy-haired elf flipped the page of his book and pretended to go back to reading it.

"Me too." He pulled up his book. "If you really care, I have some solutions that can fix my problem."

"Does it involve offing myself?" Paris asked, mock curiosity on her face.

"It might," he chirped, flipping the page of his book, not appearing to have read any of it. "But it will probably be painless for you, and best of all, your existence will stop annoying me."

"Why is it that you loathe me so, again?" Paris questioned.

"You were born," he stated.

"He's jealous because Papa dotes on Liv so much, especially after you were born," Mama Jamba stated from the corner where she was sitting quite relaxed in a pink armchair, sipping tea from a floral teacup. She was wearing a lavender velour tracksuit, and her big Dallas hair was perfectly in place, making a nice high wave over her head. Mother Nature looked out of place in the Fantastical Armory with all its weapons and strange artifacts.

"I'm not jealous," Subner argued. "I don't understand what's such a big deal about a magician who overuses sarcasm and has a child who everyone worships."

Paris stuck her hands on her hips. "No one worships me."

"Oh, yes they do," Mama Jamba countered. "As they should. You're the only halfling magician and fairy to ever exist, and to top it off, your demon blood makes you a real treasure. You're unique and destined for great things that will save this planet—bringing love to millions. Well, that is if you overcome the many challenges ahead of you and make the right choices along the way."

"So no pressure then?" Paris remarked dryly.

"You see, she does it too," Subner complained. "Sarcasm isn't funny. It's a mode of communication that highlights your passive-aggressiveness."

"If it helps, I can insult instead of being sarcastic so I'm directly aggressive," Paris joked. "Will that make you feel better?"

"I don't think there's anything you can do to make me feel better," Subner muttered. "Well, you can off yourself, as we previously discussed, but I'm guessing you're not considering that."

"As I previously discussed, Paris is destined for great things that will save this planet—bringing love to millions," Mama Jamba stated. "So I'm against the idea of her offing herself. Maybe you can eat a cookie to make you feel better, Subner."

He flipped the page of his book, again not seeming to have read any of the words. "It will have to be a really good cookie."

Mama Jamba twirled her hand, and a plate of still-steaming cookies appeared. "Those chocolate chip cookies are out of this world. I made them myself."

A smile broke across Subner's face as he took in the plate piled high with cookies. "Thanks, Mama."

"You're welcome," she sang and patted the chair next to where she sat and smiled at Paris. "Now, why don't you have a seat and enjoy a cup of tea with me, my dear. I understand you need my help with something."

Paris strode over, taking in the dainty table with the china tea set sitting between the pink armchairs. "Thank you. And yes. I need some land for my final project at Happily Ever After College. Aunt Sophia said you might be able to help me."

"I'm considering it." Mama Jamba set down her teacup. "Now go ahead and tell me the name of this restaurant you're starting."

Paris blinked at her, suddenly feeling like the woman was testing her. "I haven't come up with one yet."

Mama Jamba nodded as if she expected this answer. "Well, then the answer is no. I can't give someone a piece of fertile land if I don't know what they're going to call their business."

"I guess you're not so special after all," Subner stated through a mouthful of crumbs.

"Wait, you won't give me the land because I don't have a name for the restaurant yet?" Paris questioned. "What if I come up with one quickly?"

"Well, make it good," Mama Jamba answered. "I must know the name to decide where the land will be, and that will dictate what it will grow and the animals you'll have."

"Oh, that makes sense, I guess." Paris scratched her head, thinking of the concept she had for the farm-to-table restaurant. She wanted it to feel like everyone's home but like their dream home. It was supposed to have that homey feel with the garden and animals. It was also supposed to have a magical flair to it, as if the patrons were stepping into another land where only good things happened. "How about Backyard Bowls?"

Mama Jamba considered this. "I can offer you half an acre of land in Kentucky with a name like that."

"Kentucky?" Paris asked, not as excited about a farm-to-table restaurant in such a place. "I'm not sure that half an acre will be enough for what I'm planning."

"Then maybe you have a different name," Mama Jamba suggested. "What kinds of animals were you planning on having on this farm?"

"Well, goats for sure," Paris answered.

"Then how about the Demonic Goat," Subner offered.

"With a name like that, I'll give you an acre in Greenland," Mama Jamba sang.

"No," Paris said at once.

"And the types of foods you'll specialize in?" Mama Jamba picked up a white linen napkin and dabbed the side of her mouth.

"I was thinking light, refreshing foods like salads, sandwiches, and fruity desserts," Paris answered. "Things that are uplifting and make good use of our local ingredients, but also have a unique spin. Like twenty-four-carat beet salads with edible gold leaf garnishes and spinach and goat cheese crepes served on an encrusted walnut plate that's also edible."

"How about Planet of the Crepe?" Subner offered with a dry laugh.

"With a name like that, I'll give you two acres of land in Sudan," Mama Jamba said as if they had a bidding war.

Paris shook her head as Papa Creola entered the Fantastical Armory. He was wearing his usual tie-dye shirt with a hippie phrase on it. This one said, "Be Kind to Yourself, Tiger. You Are the King of the Jungle."

"Do you want me to save you some time and give you the name?" Papa Creola strode over to where Paris and Mama Jamba were seated.

It wasn't like Father Time to be helpful, Paris thought. Her mother said he often used riddles and made her job full of guess work as his right-hand helper.

"Yes, that would be lovely." Paris was relieved and suddenly paranoid. "Wait, why are you trying to save me time? What do I need to be doing instead of being here?"

"Besides setting up a huge business that normally would take years of hard work?" Papa Creola countered.

"Yes, besides that," Paris muttered dryly, again feeling like she'd bitten off more than she could chew, but she'd already committed at this point. She only needed the land—and a few small miracles.

"I need you to give this to Queen Helena MacGillie." He withdrew a small envelope from the back pocket of his cut-off jean shorts.

Paris again was confused. "Queen Helena MacGillie? You mean the queen of the Seelie court?"

"She's not as stupid as she looks." Subner took another bite of a cookie.

"Yes, that's who I need you to give this to." Papa Creola handed her the letter. He'd sealed it with a blue bit of wax that had Father Time's insignia on it.

"I'm not seeing the Seelie queen," Paris argued. "Fairy godmothers aren't allowed in her court."

"True," Papa Creola stated. "So give her this when you see her."

"Okay," Paris drew out the word, turning the note over. On the reverse side, he'd simply addressed it to Queen Helena MacGillie.

"The name of your restaurant is Little Pleasures," Papa Creola stated with confidence.

"Oh, I like that." Paris smiled, thinking that the name fit her goal for the restaurant.

"With a name like that, I can offer you one hundred acres in Colorado," Mama Jamba stated with a smile that made her periwinkle blue eyes dazzle.

"That would be perfect!" Paris exclaimed.

"It will be," Mama Jamba agreed. "The land is extremely fertile and has been resting for a hundred years. It will be ideal for growing lush vegetables and fruits. The amount of land is right for what you have planned, and the restaurant will have views of the Rocky Mountains."

"Thank you!" Paris clapped, careful not to bend the note.

"You're welcome, my dear," Mama Jamba said proudly. "Now, before you run off to be Papa's courier, why don't you go see Astrid. She'll have some seeds that will be perfect for your crops. Tell her I sent you. That will get you permission to get what you need, but you'll still have to secure the payment on your own."

Paris nodded, remembering that Astrid didn't take money. She only took trade for items in her horticulture and florist shop. The last and only time, it had been quite the expedition to get what she wanted —which was always specific and depended on her mood, current situation, and what she'd had for breakfast today.

Paris regarded the note in her hand and hoped that Astrid had a good and simple breakfast, making her job easier securing whatever she wanted in payment. It appeared that on top of getting this business set up, she was going to have another unexpected adventure that would somehow include meeting the Seelie queen.

CHAPTER TWELVE

Roya Lane was buzzing with excitement when Paris made her way to the Glowing Orchid. She kept her head low, not wanting to be delayed by a conversation with a random person. Growing up on Roya Lane, Paris knew many of the people on the magical avenue. Although her recent experience learning about the Glowing Orchid and the Psychic Superstore demonstrated that there were still parts of Roya Lane she didn't know about. It was always changing and full of mystery.

The Glowing Orchid smelled of fresh flowers with notes of an exotic herb Paris couldn't identify.

"Hello, Paris Beaufont." Astrid greeted her with a smile when she entered the shop. She looked past her as if expecting someone else to be with her. "Hemingway not with you today?"

Paris shook her head, trying to keep her disappointment about Hemingway leaving the college off her face. She wasn't upset at Astrid for offering him the job, although she wanted to be mad at someone. The truth was, he was the right person for the position. It was perfect for him, and it would offer him the opportunity to see the world finally—the problem was that it would take him away from her world.

"He's at the college," Paris replied. "Mama Jamba sent me to retrieve some seeds for a vegetable and fruit garden I'm having planted. She didn't tell me exactly what I needed, only to tell you that she gives her permission."

Astrid beamed with delight. "I've been looking for someone to test those new seeds. They'll be perfect for your garden."

"What are they?" Paris realized that she should probably know more about these mystery seeds she was getting.

The horticulturist snapped her fingers, and several packets appeared in her other hand. "They are a new and improved seed that grows foods faster, with enhanced nutrition and of course, better taste."

"Wow, that sounds perfect."

"They come in many different varieties." Astrid sorted through the various packets. "I've got zucchini squash, tomatoes, potatoes, celery, cucumbers, green beans, and that's only naming a few. I also have seeds for dozens of fruits."

"Thank you," Paris exclaimed, then tilted her head with hesitation. "However, all of those are probably pretty valuable. What will you need in return for them?'

"I'll keep it simple since it sounds like you're on a worthy mission," Astrid began. "Seeing you reminded me of Hemingway, who I want to treat right. Employees who are cared for work harder and smarter."

"He'll do great for you no matter what." Paris again tried to let her disappointment not surface.

"I'm certain of it," Astrid replied. "Still, I'd like to treat him with a magical cake that celebrates us working together."

Paris drew in a breath, nodding. "So you want me to go to the Crying Cat Bakery, I'm guessing…"

Astrid smiled. "That's right, and since you know Hemingway well, you'll know what kind of cake he'll like and how he'll want it decorated. Go all-out and make him something that will have him excited."

"Okay." This didn't sound as complicated as Paris had expected. She had to have a cake made for Hemingway. Ideas were already springing to her mind of things he'd like on it. However, a side trip to the Crying Cat Bakery would be full of distractions and drains on her time.

That was probably why Papa Creola had helped supply the name for her restaurant. She wasn't going to take Willow to the vortex door until the next day in the evening with Sophia and Lunis—which is when she suspected she'd be giving the Seelie queen the letter from Father Time. That meant she had the rest of the day to go on a wild goose chase, ordering cakes and doing whatever else she needed to get the business venture going.

"I know you're good for it, so I'll give you these seeds now." Astrid strode over and handed Paris the packets. "I suspect even though they're fast-growing, you'll need to get to planting right away."

"Thanks, and yes, I do." Paris had set up a time with Mama Jamba to see the plot of land in Colorado soon. She was so excited that everything was coming together. It seemed that when Paris was on the right path, things happened to support her mission. She hoped that was the case, and Little Pleasures was part of her destiny to help spread love.

"When the cake is ready, please have it sent here," Astrid continued. "I'd like to be the one to give it to Hemingway on the day he starts working for me."

Paris nodded, hoping that the cake took forever to make. She'd have to make the design extra complicated.

CHAPTER THIRTEEN

Loud, French words could be heard from inside the Crying Cat Bakery before Paris entered. She didn't want to walk in on another one of Lee's and Cat's battles. The last time, a loaf of French bread hurled through the air in her direction had nearly taken her out. Cat had aimed it at Lee, but Paris was in the path, and Cat didn't seem to care if she took out the innocent in an attempt to hit her wife.

Paris knew that mostly the fighting was for the two bakers' amusement. They seemed to enjoy insulting each other and making their patrons scared for their lives. There were probably some who visited the bakery to see what antics were happening behind the pastry display case.

"I know that you're cursing me out even if I don't speak French," Lee said to her wife when Paris entered the Crying Cat Bakery, ready to duck from flying objects. The assassin was wearing an apron covered in flour and a particularly amused expression. Conversely, Cat wore an annoyed look and no apron but had flour on her black blouse.

"Oh, funny because when I ask you to do something in English, you can't understand me," Cat retorted, her hands on her hips.

"Hey there," Paris dared to say, looking between the two who were facing off behind the counter, both of them shooting angry looks at each other.

"Can't you see we're busy?" Lee didn't take her eyes off Cat.

"I can see you're arguing," Paris stated. "All of Roya Lane can hear you."

"Serves them right for constantly annoying us by coming in here," Cat muttered, her thick French accent making it hard to understand her.

"You mean when customers come in here to buy things?" Paris asked.

Lee sighed. "Yeah, that's super annoying. They're always coming in here and asking how fresh the bread is or ordering a specialty cake. I swear I'll murder on the spot the next person who asks for one."

Paris nodded, thinking that was about right based on her usual luck. "Great. Well, sharpen your knives because I'm here to order a cake for Astrid at the Glowing Orchid."

"Oh, Astrid wants a cake?" Cat asked. "We'll do it for her. She's one of our best suppliers."

"Well, technically it's for Hemingway, but she wants me to order it," Paris explained.

"Hemingway?" Lee asked. "Didn't I murder him?"

Paris shook her head. "No, I think King Rudolf put a hit out on him but then canceled it."

"Well, do you want me to murder him?" the assassin baker asked. "Then I don't have to make the cake, and we can go and get drunk instead."

"What do you mean, get drunk?" Cat asked. "Don't you mean, get drunker?"

"You do." Lee looked Paris over. "Hey, the seventies called, and they want their leather jacket back."

Paris laughed. "I stole it from your mom."

"Your mom goes to college," Cat said as if that made any sense at all.

"Oh, good, are we doing *Napoleon Dynamite* references?" Lee asked.

"Tina, you fat lard. Come and get some dinner." She glanced at Paris. "Okay, your turn."

"Maybe later," Paris answered. "I need to order that cake. Also, I'm opening a restaurant. I wondered if you wanted to supply the pastries, bread, and some of the desserts."

"No, no, and no." Lee crossed her arms over her chest.

"Oh, well, I would give you one hundred percent of the profits from sales for them," Paris reasoned. "The restaurant isn't about making money."

"Neither is our bakery," Lee stated.

"It's how we launder money," Cat added.

"And hide the assassin business," Lee said.

Paris laughed, amused. "Which, by the way, you probably shouldn't talk about so much if it's supposed to be a secret."

Lee rolled her eyes. "How else are we going to get customers? We thrive on word-of-mouth referrals."

"Are you starting an assassin business too?" Cat asked. "Is that what the restaurant is a front for?"

"No, it's to promote love," Paris answered.

"Murdering people promotes love," Lee argued. "I reason that by taking out horrible oafs that clog our streets with their stupidity, I've created a lot of love around the world."

"Your reasoning is sound," Paris muttered. "Seriously, I think offering some of your products in my restaurant will be good. Magical pastries that make people happier or tarts that bring bliss."

"What's in it for me?" Lee asked.

Paris lowered her chin and drew in an impatient breath. "Again, you get one hundred percent of the profits."

"But I have to do one hundred percent of the work, and you know how I feel about work," Lee stated.

"She doesn't like it," Cat offered. "I'm certain that lifting a finger to do something might kill her." She glanced intently at Lee. "Hey, let's put that to the test. Pick something up and let's see if it kills you."

"How about that knife?" Lee pointed at a large meat cleaver precariously stuck into a sack of flour, its handle protruding from the top. "Then we can play that fun game where we toss it back and forth. Try and see if you can catch it without using your hands."

"You two are adorable," Paris teased.

"Take that back, or I'm not going into business with you," Lee threatened.

"So, you're going to supply the bread and stuff for my restaurant?" Paris asked, hope in her tone.

"Of course, I will," Lee answered. "You're a Beaufont. If I don't do everything you say, your dragon will chomp my head off."

"That's Sophia, my aunt, who has the dragon."

"Well, then your little lynx will curse me and leave turds in my bed," Lee stated.

"That's my mom who has Plato," Paris argued. "I'm the one with the talking squirrel as a sidekick."

"Just do whatever she asks," Cat said to Lee in a mad rush, fear covering her face. "We can't afford to anger the gods."

"The gods?" Paris was confused.

"Everyone knows that centuries ago, the gods took the form of squirrels," Lee explained.

"Not everyone knows that," Paris remarked. "I don't think Faraday is a god. More like an awkward nerd."

"If he has a tail and chirps like a squirrel, he's a god," Lee replied. "Don't worry. You'll get your stuff for the restaurant. Now tell me about this cake you want."

Paris drew in a breath. "I want something big and complicated that takes eons to make. Maybe something that needs to be fermented or aged."

"For how long?" Cat asked.

Paris blew out the air in her lungs with a sigh. "Preferably years."

CHAPTER FOURTEEN

"Swallow it and see if it kills you," King Rudolf Sweetwater ordered Ramy Vance when Paris entered Heals Pills. Sophia had suggested that she sell some of the store's healing products in the restaurant at the boutique front. It was a brilliant idea, and Paris thought it would increase the love factor.

"It smells bad though," Ramy complained, pinching his nose.

Sitting between the two men on the countertop were mushrooms of different sizes, shapes, and colors.

King Rudolf pressed a brown mushroom in Ramy's face. "Just do it. I need to figure out which one is which."

"What are y'all doing?" Paris asked skeptically.

"I collected a bunch of magical mushrooms from this special forest," King Rudolf explained. "Some have healing properties. Some make you hallucinate. One is poisonous. Ramy-Cans is helping me figure out which one is which."

Ramy pointed at a flat white mushroom. "That one causes hallucination. Unless you hired a monkey to sing to me while hanging from the ceiling, King Rudolf."

"Not today, I didn't," he answered.

Paris chuckled. "Well, before you die—"

SARAH NOFFKE & MICHAEL ANDERLE

"I hoped not to today," Ramy interrupted with a tired sigh.

"Oh, would you stop being such a baby," the fae ordered. "You can't be killed—"

"Easily," Ramy cut in.

King Rudolf nodded. "You can't be killed easily, and you always return, much to my dismay sometimes. You might as well put your powers to good use. We're running out of Heals Pills, and since there are no more dragon eggs shells, the main ingredient in our formula, we need a replacement. Eat a potentially poisonous mushroom already." He shoved the brown mushroom in Ramy's direction again.

"About Heals Pills," Paris cut in. Ramy gave her a relieved look, grateful for her interruption. "I'm opening a restaurant and hoped to sell some of your products in the front."

"No can do," King Rudolf stated. "Our products are exclusively sold here so we control the market and pricing. It was one of Sophia's main rules when we set up the business."

"It was Sophia's idea that I sell the products," Paris explained.

Rudolf sputtered out a sigh. "Well, then you'll have to get a meeting between Past Sophia and Present Sophia and have them resolve this inconsistency in the rule."

"I think Present Sophia trumps past Sophia," Paris offered.

"I guess you're right," Rudolf replied. "Don't get me started on the stuff that Past Rudolf does to me. I swear, every morning, I'm piecing together the crimes he's left behind for me to solve or cover up. He's a real pill, that guy."

"He's you." Paris laughed.

King Rudolf gave her a look of offense. "He is not. He's who I used to be. I'm much wiser than the guy who I was a moment ago. Or a second ago. Or the guy who just said that." The fae puffed out his chest and looked around proudly. "I'm much better than I used to be."

"Well, tell Past Rudolf that I'd like Future Rudolf to deliver some of your Heals Pills products to my new restaurant," Paris stated. "I'm going to visit it tomorrow and will send you over the address once I have it."

The king of the fae crossed his arms over his chest. "I'm not talking to Past Rudolf. He hid all the blueberry wine and won't tell me where it is."

"Are you sure you didn't drink it and forgot?" Ramy asked.

Rudolf picked up the mushroom he'd set down and shoved it in Ramy's face. "Eat this and tell me how you feel."

"Fine." Ramy sighed. He took the mushroom and popped it in his mouth, chewing fast and swallowing. "It doesn't taste that bad. That queasy feeling in my stomach from the hallucinogen mushroom is starting to ease."

"Oh, good," Rudolf chirped. "Then that has to be the healing one. Looks like you don't have to eat the last one."

"Great!" Ramy exclaimed. "I don't have to die today."

"The people in my life are so weird," Paris muttered.

No one heard her though, because Ramy yelped like he was suddenly in pain. He clutched his stomach—his face blossoming into a violent shade of red. "I spoke too soon. That mushroom is definitely poison."

Once again, Paris watched as Ramy Vance keeled over, falling to the floor on his face—dead.

King Rudolf sighed and rolled his eyes. "Well, at least we know which mushroom is which."

Paris shook her head. "Maybe this time his death wasn't senseless and avoidable and will lead to something good."

"Oh, I knew which mushroom was which," Rudolf stated. "I wanted to watch Ramy-Cans hallucinate. Then I needed him out of my hair. Papa needs a nap, and I can never get one with that guy around."

"Wow, that's dark," Paris commented. "You killed your friend to get some quiet time."

He shrugged. "I've done much worse when I needed a nap. Now turn the lights off when you leave. It's sleepy time for me."

"Night, Ru," Paris sang, heading for the door, not wanting to be another of the fae's casualties when he was sleepy.

CHAPTER FIFTEEN

"I don't even know what to say." Paris gasped, looking at the raw and fertile lands given to her near Boulder, Colorado, by Mama Jamba. The Rocky Mountains provided a magnificent backdrop to the green lands flecked with wildflowers and grass blowing in the wind, like waves on the ocean.

"You can start with 'thank you.'" Mother Nature surveyed the area around them with a wide and proud smile.

"Well, of course, thank you," Paris remarked, once again overwhelmed by the tasks she'd taken upon herself. She knew that it was a huge undertaking, creating a farm and building a restaurant, but now looking at the untouched land, she wondered if her dream was possible in the time permitted to her or with an unending time allowance. It seemed like something that experts and families and those not raised in a vacuum could pull off—not Paris Beaufont.

"I didn't expect something so grand," Paris stated, feeling breathless.

"Well, if it doesn't suit your goals, then rename the restaurant and farm, and I'll give you something more suitable." Mama Jamba hid a sneaky grin. "I have some unused land on the outskirts of Detroit you might like."

Paris shook her head. "I highly doubt that."

Kneeling a few yards away, Hemingway let a clump of moist soil slip through his hand to the earth where it had come from. "The land is perfect. Not only will everything grow here and thrive, but the seeds you have from Astrid will grow fast."

Paris nodded, feeling marginally better by this news. "I like the idea that the foods we grow will have enhanced nutrition."

"The land is perfect, as I assured you," Mama Jamba imparted. "It's been resting for a century for expressly these purposes."

Paris looked sideways at the short woman, who was unassuming and also intimidating as hell. "Do you mean that you put this land aside because you knew one day I'd need it for Little Pleasures farm and restaurant?"

Mother Nature rocked forward on her tiptoes and back again. "Maybe."

"I can start planting the garden," Hemingway cut in, arching an eyebrow at the coy answer given by Mama Jamba. "But as I said before, I can't manage it going forward."

Paris nodded, the heavy feeling returning. She hadn't yet tackled the employment challenge, although she knew that would be a big part of getting the business running and continuously operating. She knew that to get things off the ground, so to speak, she needed the help of experts.

People like Mama Jamba for the land, Astrid for the seeds, Hemingway for the farm, and Chef Ash for the restaurant menu. They all had other responsibilities and would need to turn things over to full-time employees inevitably. Again, Paris was out of her comfort zone. People went to college to learn how to manage restaurants.

Not only did Paris not have the first clue about how to craft a business plan or balance its budget, but human resource management was a term that gave her hives. She had no idea what a criminal, avoiding jail and going to fairy godmother college instead, was doing launching a huge business.

However, Mama Jamba had set aside this land for her over a hundred years ago. Paris was supposed to do great things...well, if she made the right decisions and whatever random things she needed to do along the way. It was all a Choose Your Own Adventure riddle that kept her befuddled and second-guessing herself constantly.

No, Paris was charging ahead and having faith that the right people would come along to help. She knew people who knew people, and hopefully, it was only a matter of time before everything fell into place. *That was faith, right,* she reasoned.

"I know," Paris gave Hemingway a meaningful look. "Thank you. Anything you can do will help."

"You need him to till the soil and start the crops," Mama Jamba said in a firm tone.

Blinking at the blue-haired woman, Paris smiled. "Are you going to tell me why?"

"Not yet." Mama Jamba rocked up and back on her heels.

Paris nodded, having expected this answer.

Chef Ash hurried over with an excited grin. He had his trusty pencil out from behind his ear and sketched on a pad as he walked. "I think I've deduced the perfect spot for the restaurant." With the tip of the yellow pencil, he indicated an area next to a stand of thick trees. "That shelterbelt will provide coverage from high winds and also a nice view of the sunset over the mountains. It should make for an ideal dining experience."

"That's exactly where the old farmhouse restaurant should go," Mama Jamba confirmed.

Chef Ash blinked at her with sudden surprise before turning around his pad to show a two-story house with shutters and a wrap-around porch. "I was going to suggest the restaurant be an old farm-house style. Something that has the charm of simpler days but with all our magical conveniences. How did you know?"

Hemingway chuckled. "She's Mother Nature. She probably knows what your children's names will be."

Mama Jamba shook her head. "Those names aren't set in stone as of yet, but please take it under advisement that Gray is no name for a girl if you want her to have a personality."

Chef Ash grimaced. "Gray? Why would I name my daughter Gray?"

"Because your wife said so," Mama Jamba answered.

"An Old World-style farmhouse sounds lovely," Paris cut in, trying to steer the conversation back on track. "Do you think that after you draw up the plans, you can build it if you employ magic?"

Chef Ash laughed. "I'm a lot of things, but an expert builder who can expedite projects of this magnitude isn't one. I can create the plans and start the work, but unfortunately, I can't see it to completion. Especially with the work I need to do on the menu for the restaurant."

Paris nodded, also having expected this answer. What could she do, though? It was a lot to ask of her friends, but she did need their help with starting the projects. "Well, I'll have to figure something out..."

"I think you might have some help there." Mama Jamba winked at Paris.

She drew in a breath, wondering what riddle she'd have to untangle next to find this help. "Yeah, I know that Aunt Sophia said she'd try and enlist some help. It seems I might need an army to get this job done."

"Not an army," Mama Jamba corrected. "Just the best of the very best. It looks like they're all arriving now." She nodded toward Paris' back, a glint of a smile in her eyes.

Paris saw a shimmering light behind her and turned to find what she expected—a portal. However, the first person who stepped through wasn't at all who she would've expected to join them there in an open field in Colorado.

CHAPTER SIXTEEN

The giant had to duck to come through the large oval opening. The light shimmering from the portal made it hard to see the expression on Rory Lauren's face until he was all the way through. However, like the last time Paris had seen him, he had a neutral expression. Much like gnomes and Wilfred, the AI magitech butler, the giant, like most of his kind, hardly smiled.

A moment later, arriving beside him was a giantess who Paris didn't recognize. In contrast to Rory, she wore a genuine smile, and her eyes were full of wonder as she looked around the fields and the mountains in the distance.

The giantess was roughly the same age as Rory, but Paris didn't know what that translated to based on how giants matured. They didn't age as slowly as magicians, fairies, and the fae. The giantess had long blonde hair pulled back into pigtails and wore overalls, making her appear to be a farmer.

"Rory?" Paris looked between Mama Jamba and the giant. "What's he doing here?"

"Giants are excellent builders," Mama Jamba stated. "Not only because they're strong, but because they connect to the Earth element.

That makes them excellent gardeners too, but I have someone else lined up for caring for your grounds."

"You do?" Paris was shocked and excited at the same time.

Mama Jamba shooed her forward. "I don't need to make introductions for you, dear. Go on and do that on your own as everyone arrives. They've all willingly signed up for this venture, so please make them feel welcome."

"Of course." Paris rushed forward, smiling wide at the two giants. "Hi! You've come to help me with my farm and restaurant?"

Rory nodded, glancing around at the property. "Yes, and a fine piece of land this will be for such a project."

"Thank you." Paris turned her attention to the still smiling giantess. "I'm Paris Beaufont."

The giantess blinked sweetly down at her. "I know that. I knew you as a baby, but you wouldn't remember that. I'm Maddy, Rory's wife. I've been away helping my papa with his barbeque restaurant in Texas but recently returned. I heard you needed some help and couldn't think of a better project for us. A farm-to-table restaurant sounds perfect, and I love the idea of it bringing love to so many."

Paris tried to keep the look of surprise off her face. It was just that in comparison to the other giants she'd met, Maddy was...nice. Usually, they were mean or bad-tempered. At least the ones on Roya Lane who she'd had to put in their places for bullying others had been. There was Bermuda Laurens, who wasn't the angry type but was serious. Rory was less so, and according to Liv, a bit untraditional in comparison to other giants in that he enjoyed the arts—writing novels.

"Wow, thank you," Paris beamed. "So you have restaurant experience then?"

Maddy nodded, pressing one of her pigtails behind her ear. "I sure do. I grew up helping my papa, and I know the ins and outs of running a restaurant."

Paris couldn't believe this. "Mama Jamba said you two were here to help with the building because that was part of your expertise, but maybe you'll be willing to help me with restaurant knowledge? Pretty please."

"I'm going to do most of the building," Rory cut in. "With the help of someone who is an expert in renovation magic, of course. It's not something that giants employ a lot because we prefer to make things with our hands. For a project like this, you're going to need the building to be magical in a few different ways."

Maddy nodded. "Although I'm going to help with building, after we finish, well, I hoped to hang around."

Paris blinked at her in surprise. The question was obvious on her face—at least she hoped.

"To help with service, of course," Maddy supplied. "You're going to need a waitress, right?"

"Of course!" Paris exclaimed. "You have so much experience. That would be amazing."

"Los Angeles, where we live, is nice," Rory added, "but I think we're ready for a change in scenery. So when Mama Jamba offered to give us a piece of property adjacent to yours, I couldn't resist."

Maddy threaded her arm through her husband's and laid her head on his shoulder. "The fresh mountain air will be perfect for Rory—inspiring his next novel."

"Oh that sounds wonderful," Paris offered, so happy that her venture was going to create opportunities for others. Wasn't that the best business? Something that brought love to its patrons and offered value to those connected.

"It's about aliens in Colorado," Maddy stated proudly, looking affectionately at Rory.

He blushed. "I thought the scenery might help me with the words."

"I hope so," Paris remarked. "Thank you so much. This is incredible."

"Giants are perfect for this project." Chef Ash strode forward, holding up his sketch pad. "I'm working on the preliminary design."

He offered it to Rory, who glanced over it, nodding. "Yes, we can make this happen. We'll craft the farmhouse restaurant, then work on a cabin on our property. Maybe you can help us with a design for that? This is great work."

Chef Ash smiled wide. "I'd be beyond honored. I could make something that blends into the scenery."

"That would be ideal." Rory held out his hand. "I'm Rory Laurens, and this is my wife, Maddy Laurens."

The chef and architect held out his hand. "Ashton Maxwell at your service. But everyone calls me Chef Ash." He looked up at the giantess. "It's wonderful to know that Paris can rely on your restaurant expertise. I'll be crafting the menu."

"Seems that we have a lot of fun work to do," Maddy said in an excited voice.

"That we do," Rory stated. "I think we should start the building right away. I'll get right to ordering supplies for this design."

"I'll show you the area I picked for the house," Chef Ash added, leading the other two in the direction of the trees.

"Yes, but you mentioned something about someone who would help with renovation magic," Paris interrupted, pausing the three.

Rory turned and nodded, pointing at the portal. "Yes, and it looks like he's arriving. Have him join us over here once he's all the way through and ready."

Paris turned to the portal to find another unexpected face greeting her.

CHAPTER SEVENTEEN

"Uncle Clark!" Paris ran forward, throwing her arms around the guy who stepped through the portal, appearing disoriented as he took in his surroundings.

He wrapped his arms around her, holding her tightly. "Good to see you, Paris."

She stepped back, blinking up at him. Like every time she'd seen him, his blond hair was slicked back, not a strand out of place. He was also wearing his usual black starched suit with a tie as if he'd come from a business meeting. More likely, he'd been attending to House of Fourteen business or rolled out of bed looking like that. Paris thought that Uncle Clark wore a suit as his pajamas.

"You're an expert in renovation magic?" Paris asked. She wasn't sure why this was a surprise. Maybe because Uncle Clark was so obsessed with reading and research that she didn't take him as an expert in the practical application of magic. He'd seemed like a knower rather than a doer.

"Who do you think created Liv's apartment above John's Repair Shop?" he asked.

Paris thought about the huge penthouse apartment where Uncle Clark lived that had also been her home with her parents when she was young. It was big enough for all four of them. Actually, the sprawling apartment with beautiful pillars and chandeliers was big enough for ten people to live in.

It had oversized balconies for taking in the Hollywood sunsets and a huge kitchen where Uncle Clark made many of his feasts. The ceilings were at least twenty feet tall, and he'd paid unique attention to so many parts of the apartment that Paris hadn't been able to explore all of them.

"You renovated the apartment?" Paris asked, not sure what all that meant. Was Uncle Clark responsible for the stark white walls and matching shiny marble floors? Or was his design eye what put the wrought iron railing around the balcony?

"I sure did," Clark answered. "Before, it was a one-bedroom studio that was almost too small for Liv and Plato."

Paris' mouth dropped open. "Wait, that's all renovation magic? So is it all glamour? I don't understand how our apartment is so large."

He smiled modestly. "Magic, of course. But it's a special brand. Similar to the House of Fourteen or Happily Ever After mansion or the Castle at the Gullington or the Great Library or your Bewilder Forest, it's alive. We're not only going to build a house. I think it's better to think of it as growing a house. That way, we can change it but also remember that means it will be an organic being with its own ideas and constantly adapting based on different factors."

"Wow, that sounds complicated," Paris stated.

"Yes, thankfully, you'll have two experts running the restaurant and grounds who are experts at dealing with a place full of similar magic," Uncle Clark stated.

"I will?" Paris questioned, trying to think of who she knew who matched that description. "I don't know who that could be..."

He nodded as if this made perfect sense to him. "That's because you haven't met them yet."

Turning back to the portal as though he'd planned the timing, Uncle Clark held out his arm to the shimmering air as a short figure followed by a taller, willowy one stepped through. "It looks like they're arriving now."

CHAPTER EIGHTEEN

Uncle Clark didn't hang around to help make introductions. Once he caught sight of Rory, Maddy, and Chef Ash in the distance, he strode in their direction, saying something over his shoulder about needing to get right to work.

Paris suddenly felt nervous as a small gnome with strangely wise eyes and a tall elf woman with red hair approached from the portal. She didn't know why but felt like she was in the presence of very old and wise beings. That feeling immediately evaporated when the elf spoke.

"Do you wear all black because of your demon blood?" the woman asked, her Irish accent thick. She wore a smart brown dress made of burlap, and although it appeared durable, its style was very fashionable, the hem hitting her mid-calf and the sleeves three-quarter length.

Paris tilted her head, not sure exactly how to respond. "I don't think so. Mostly it's because I don't want decision fatigue. I wear the same thing every single day to keep things easy."

The gnome muttered beside the elf, and she nodded as if she understood him perfectly, although Paris couldn't understand a word he said.

"I agree." The woman again nodded at the gnome, who was much shorter than her. "She should at least launder the clothes once in a while. I hope she does."

Paris chuckled, wondering what circus show she'd been invited to and where these freaks had come from. "I have multiple black shirts and pants. I even change my undies and socks every day."

The gnome, who wore a brown knit cap pulled down on his chubby face, mumbled something again that was inaudible.

The elf pursed her lips at Paris before glancing down at the small man. "I know. I'm not sure we needed that much information either. People's undergarments should remain their business and not ours."

Deciding that she was probably overdue for introductions, Paris extended her hand between the two. "Well, I sense you already know me since you know about my demon blood, but I'm Paris Beaufont. It's nice to meet you…whoever you are."

"Didn't your Aunt Sophia tell you about us?" the redhead asked. "We're legendary and known far and wide—throughout history and chronicled in every history book ever to be written. I'm Ainsley Carter, and this is MacAfee Gullington, but we call him Quiet."

Drawing in a breath, Paris tried to think of a polite way to respond. "I guess I need to brush up on my history. I haven't heard of either of you."

Ainsley blinked at Paris as though she misheard her. "Are you certain? My name is Ainsley with a 'Y,' but sometimes I'm referred to as Ains. Oh, and there was that one time the history book called me by some very rude names."

"Again, I'm not real well-read," Paris admitted. "I spent the majority of my life sheltered."

Ainsley scoffed. "Try spending five hundred years locked in a castle."

Quiet muttered again, his voice barely a whisper.

The elf glanced down at him. "Yes, of course, you made it very nice. It's just that after a century of Old World charm, anyone would want to jump off the highest turret."

Paris nodded in the direction of the gnome, who wore pants to match his knit hat and a button-up plaid shirt. His cheeks were rosy, and he looked much nicer than the gambling gnomes she usually met and put in their places on Roya Lane. "What did he say?"

Ainsley's mouth popped open with offense. "It was clear as day. How did you not hear it? Maybe you need to have your ears checked."

"I think my ears are fine," Paris argued. "I mean, you said his name is also Quiet. Is that because he speaks so softly?"

The gnome made more of a grunting sound than mumbled this time.

Ainsley nodded. "Not the brightest Beaufont, but S. Beaufont says that she's noble and brave, so we're going to help her out."

Quiet murmured in reply.

"Well, true that," Ainsley retorted at once, looking around. "I'm here for the break in scenery and new adventure too. But we're getting points for being helpful, and none will be the wiser that we have our own interests driving us."

"You said that out loud." Paris laughed, wondering if this was all a joke, set up for Mama Jamba's amusement or something. The older woman was watching from a distance, Paris noticed from her peripheral vision, catching Mother Nature's amused expression from the corner of her eye.

"Are you sure?" Ainsley challenged, arching an eyebrow at her.

Paris blinked, not having expected that response. "At this point, I'm not totally sure. Maybe I've imagined all of this, and you're both a figment of my imagination."

Ainsley nodded before glancing down at the gnome. "Yes, I think this one will do just fine. We'll have a lot of fun with her."

He replied, again inaudible.

The elf scowled back at him and folded her arms. "You're no fun. Fine, I won't steal her clothes. But I need a new leather jacket. She wouldn't know if I took it."

Paris tugged at her jacket. "Ummm...yes, I will. And again, I'm certain you said that out loud."

"Sooooo," Ainsley began, drawing out the word. "Your aunt, S.

Beaufont, says that you're starting a produce stand on the side of the road and need our help making baskets and picking persimmons."

"It's a restaurant," Paris corrected. "This is the farm where we'll plant the crops and have the animals."

Ainsley glanced around. "Right. I must've misheard. I wasn't really listening. S. Beaufont said, you want a break from hanging around this dreary castle and watching the mundane sheep graze over the hills for hours, and I packed a bag."

Paris noticed immediately that the elf didn't have a bag.

Quiet said something that sounded like, "It's not dreary."

Ainsley turned back to him. "It wouldn't be if you didn't stop taking down my Hello Kitty posters. I think a little Japanese culture mixed with an Old World Scottish castle is what we've been missing."

Paris wanted to be relieved when Mama Jamba arrived at her side, thinking that things would suddenly start to make sense. However, she realized that was a pipedream when the old woman grinned at the pair in front of her and said, "Ains, did you bring me some pancakes?"

She smiled and curtsied. "Mama, I'll make you some as soon as someone points me in the direction of the kitchen."

Mama Jamba pointed over her shoulder to where Rory, Uncle Clark, Maddy, and Chef Ash surveyed the area where they'd build the farmhouse. "It's over there."

Ainsley glanced in that direction and grimaced. "It's a bit rustic. I was hoping for..." She snapped her fingers as if she was trying to remember something. "What's that word...oh, yeah. Electricity. Oh, and maybe some walls...and plumbing. But I guess I've worked with less."

Quiet muttered, tilting his head back and forth angrily.

Ainsley stuck her hands on her hips and glared down at the small man. "You gave me one spice rack to feed an entire clan of hungry and demanding men. One spice rack. Really?"

Paris turned to Mama Jamba and feigned a smile. "So, a tiny, small question. Who the hell are these people?"

Mama Jamba returned the smile, hers much sweeter. "This is Ainsley Carter and Quiet."

The elf turned her angry look on Paris. "She hasn't read about us in the history books."

"Which books should I reference?" Paris questioned.

"All of them!" Ainsley exclaimed, her face flushing red to match her hair.

"I'll get right on that." Paris had to stifle a laugh.

"They're in them," Mama Jamba affirmed. "It's just that you have to read in between the lines to see them referenced."

"Right." Paris drew the word out. "And these historical figures... why are they here?"

"Isn't it obvious?" Mama Jamba asked with surprise.

Paris wanted to reply that nothing was obvious about this current situation. Instead, she shook her head.

Mama Jamba grinned, looking at the pair proudly. "These two legends have been recruited to temporarily run your restaurant and grounds, of course."

CHAPTER NINETEEN

"What?" Paris received the biggest shock of the day. She realized she should've said "thank you," but she wasn't sure whether to be grateful or worried. Paris couldn't understand what Quiet said, and Ainsley made her doubt her sanity, so she was unsure if she wanted their help running the restaurant and grounds or if they were truly capable of it. Maybe Mama Jamba was messing with her or was on the decline, having finally lost her beautiful mind.

"Oh, great." Ainsley sighed. "At first she didn't understand Quiet, and now she can't understand you, Mama. I fear there's no helping this one."

Mama Jamba shook her head and smiled politely at Paris. "Ainsley and Quiet are the staff who care for the Gullington in Scotland where the Dragon Elite have their headquarters."

"The other organization where Aunt Sophia works?" Paris had heard of it but was more familiar with the mansion in Beverly Hills, California, where the Rogue Riders resided.

"That's right," Mama Jamba stated. "They've done a fine job caring for the riders for many centuries. I thought it was time they had a side adventure. Not forever, but until your business is off the ground and you find suitable replacements."

"I really appreciate that, but—"

"But you doubt their competence," Mama Jamba interrupted boldly. "As you should."

"One hundred percent," Ainsley stated. "I wouldn't employ me."

Quiet mumbled, nodding.

Mama Jamba winked at the two. "I have every confidence in them. That's why I appointed Quiet to be caretaker for the Castle and grounds of the Gullington since the beginning."

"He actually is the Castle and the grounds," Ainsley stated.

"How's that?" Paris asked.

"Well, it's a living and breathing organic being that's tethered to the consciousness of Quiet," Mama Jamba explained. "I needed to have someone, rather than something to house the Gullington for the Dragon Elite when I created the organization."

"Then is it okay for him to be here?" Paris questioned.

"Good question," Mama Jamba stated. "Yes, for the time being, everything will be fine because I've put certain provisions into place."

"Well, and the Dragon Elite is a much better position and more stable than in centuries past," Ainsley added.

Mother Nature nodded. "Yes, the chi of the dragon is very strong and a sustainable, renewable source of magic that is fueling the protective forces of the Gullington."

"As a bonus," Ainsley began, "the dragonriders get a break and don't have constant pranks pulled on them."

Quiet scowled, mumbling.

"Oh, really?" Ainsley argued. "Then how did all of Evan's possessions become individually tied to the back of the sheep in the flock?"

The gnome shrugged, feigning innocence.

Ainsley laughed though, glancing at Paris. "You should've seen poor Evan running after each sheep trying to untie his shoes or shirt or whatever from their backs. It took him the better part of an afternoon. Then they all smelled like sheep and were covered in bits of wool. Now he looks and smells like one himself."

Quiet muttered, rocking forward and back.

Ainsley nodded. "I agree, he deserved it, but still, you're quite the prankster."

"You'll be taking care of the grounds of Little Pleasures farms?" Paris asked, again doubting that this was a good idea.

"Yes, and under his care, things will run much smoother than if you have a crew of workers," Mama Jamba answered. "Once Hemingway has the crops planted, then Quiet can do the harvesting and tending. He'll also take care of all the animals. You'll have nothing at all to worry about. Well, except that once you graduate from Happily Ever After College, you'll have to replace Quiet since I'll need him back at the Gullington."

"Right," Paris chirped, the idea of graduation filling her with sudden trepidation. "And Ainsley, you said she was in charge of the restaurant."

"Yes, I did," Mama Jamba affirmed, looking at the elf proudly. "Maddy will be your wait staff and this lovely shapeshifter will be your chef."

"You're a shapeshifter?" Paris asked in astonishment. She'd heard of them but had never met one.

"Yes, but I don't change on demand and usually only do it when there's some entertainment reward for me," Ainsley stated. "I enjoy torturing the riders at the Gullington as much as Quiet. It gives our lives meaning."

Paris chuckled. "Sounds like you use your powers for good."

"That I do," Ainsley sang. "The good of keeping me happy."

"Again," Mama Jamba began. "I can only give you Ainsley's help at Little Pleasures until graduation. So you'll want to keep an eye out for a replacement."

"And you have cooking experience?" Paris asked, feeling like she had to ask the question, even if Mother Nature was assigning her.

"I've been cooking for a group of ungrateful men for over five hundred years," Ainsley answered. "I think running a food truck for you will be easy as pie."

"It's a farm-to-table restaurant," Paris corrected.

"Same thing," Ainsley argued.

"Well, if you're going to be the chef, I think I should introduce you to the person designing our menu." Paris turned to where Chef Ash was still talking with Rory and Maddy Laurens.

"I'll do the honors." Mama Jamba trotted in the direction of the giants and architect and waved for Ainsley and Quiet to follow her. "You should stay and greet the last person who Sophia and I have recruited to help you."

"Oh?" Paris questioned with more surprise, turning back to the portal and wondering who would be coming through next.

For the first time all afternoon, when the person stepped through the portal, it made sense to Paris for once.

CHAPTER TWENTY

"Of course," Paris said, mostly to herself. "Animals. I'll need someone to help me with the animals."

"Of course you will," Bermuda Laurens, the expert on magical creatures stated after ducking to step through the portal—which closed immediately afterward. "When I heard about this project, I thought it would be a good opportunity to test out some new animals I've found."

"Oh?" Paris questioned. "Are they risky?"

"That's why we're testing them out, isn't it?" the giantess questioned matter-of-factly.

"Right..." Paris stated. "So you're supplying me with untested animals for my farm-to-table restaurant..."

"That I am," Bermuda answered, looking around the grounds and nodding appreciatively. "This will do fine. We can put the animal tent and pens on the opposite side of the restaurant." She pointed to where her son and the others were next to the tree line. "I'm guessing that's where that will be built then?"

Paris nodded in reply.

Bermuda then indicated where Hemingway was already at work in the field in front of them. "And that's where the crops will be planted?"

Another nod.

"Yes, then I want the animal tent and pens over there." Bermuda pointed at the opposite side from where the farmhouse was being built, also adjacent to a line of trees and also sheltered by a mountain ridge.

"Oh, that's fine, but I'm not sure when we can build that," Paris related. "Rory and the others are already maxed out building the restaurant and then the other things."

"I come bringing solutions, not more problems." Bermuda pulled something small from her pocket. She opened the palm of her hand to show a tiny circus-like tent in colors of blues like the sky overhead and green like the field below them.

Paris immediately thought of the hot air balloon that Rudolf gave her to take to Happily Ever After College. It was miniature until she performed the enlarging spell on it. "Is that charmed to be a tiny version that will blow up to a giant one?"

"Of course it is," Bermuda stated like this should have been obvious. "I'd prefer if you didn't use my race as an adjective. You wouldn't like it if I said, 'Are you having a magician day?' or 'You're a real fairy, crying all the time.'"

Paris let out a long breath. "I'm not sure what that means. What does a magician day mean?"

"Rough," Bermuda stated.

"And fairy, in that context?"

"Emotional," the giantess stated.

"Yeah, I'm not in favor of those definitions," Paris said.

"I don't make these things up," Bermuda imparted. "I simply state the obvious."

"Is it though?" Paris argued. "I don't see how the way I used giant is comparative. You are large and—"

"I think you can also use magician to describe things that are offensive," Bermuda interrupted.

"So your tent enlarges, huh?" Paris questioned at once, trying to change the subject and preserve her patience.

"Yes, and I'll bring the animals once I set it up," Bermuda answered. "Quiet will be the perfect one to tend to them."

"I hope so." Paris looked toward where the gnome and the others were already hard at work. She was still doubtful about the strange character and elf, but she trusted Mama Jamba. If she couldn't trust Mother Nature, she didn't know who she could. "What kinds of animals will you be supplying me with for the farm?"

"Ones who will be of use to you," Bermuda stated like this should have been obvious.

"I was hoping for specifics."

"Fine," Bermuda sighed. "Ones that lay eggs. Ones that give milk. And ones that supply honey."

"Oh, so chickens, goats, and bees," Paris guessed.

A look of offense jumped to Bermuda's face. "No. I'm stocking the tent with magical animals."

"That's right," Paris stated. "Ones that are untested. I look forward to this new adventure."

"You should," Bermuda replied. "Because if these three animals get along on the same farm, it will be a downright miracle."

Paris gulped. "Oh, good. It sounds like this will be a real adventure then."

"It's an experiment," Bermuda corrected. "If it all goes well, your farm and restaurant are sure to be a definite success."

"Great!" Paris smiled, feeling hopeful.

"If it doesn't," Bermuda countered. "Then this part of Colorado will be utterly destroyed."

Paris' smile faded. "Of course it will…"

CHAPTER TWENTY-ONE

P aris had seen many, many strange things in her life, living on a magical lane, then attending Happily Ever After College and learning about her family—the Beaufonts. But she'd seen nothing at all like what she was presently staring at on the Enchanted Grounds.

"How does he do that?" Paris asked her Aunt Sophia, standing next to her.

Before she could respond, the super-sized dragon responded. "I had a big dinner last night."

Sophia shook her head. "Lunis has a large dinner every night. Usually, it consists of things that have lots of preservatives and are an unnatural color."

"There's nothing wrong with having a Dorito dinner, Soph," the blue dragon argued. "If it makes you happy, it can't be that bad."

"Are we going to quote Sheryl Crow lyrics the rest of the day, or what?" Sophia joked, mildly amused.

"Hey, all I wanna do is have some fun," Lunis said plainly. "I got a feeling I'm not the only one."

Sophia sighed. "Well, this has started about the way I expected."

Paris lowered her chin and regarded the dragonrider with dry surprise. "You expected our expedition over the Bewilder Forest to start with your super-sized dragon quoting nineties pop lyrics?"

"It usually does with Lunis, especially when he takes his mega form," Sophia replied.

The majestic dragon perched on the Enchanted Grounds of Happily Ever After College taking up a considerable amount of space. He was at least the size of a 747 airplane. His connection to the moon allowed him to harness its energy and employ it at will to become enormous.

It's what he'd done when he and Faraday had to intercept and block the signal broadcasting from the satellite that made cellphones addictive. However, Paris hadn't been there for that mission—she'd been in the jail trying to stop Agent Ruby. She'd heard from the talking squirrel that Lunis' size was unbelievable but truly felt astonished on a new level as she took in his massive form.

Sophia had agreed to transport Paris and Headmistress Willow Starr to the vortex door on the other side of the Bewilder Forest and the other strange terrain. Paris' blood had created it all, which meant that yet again, she'd need to accompany Willow on the excursion. Hopefully, in time, Hemingway and the other professors would understand and tame the forest, making it safe for others. Until then, they'd decided that Paris should chaperone in case it played tricks as it had with Hemingway and Bermuda.

Even flying over the diverse lands didn't seem safe without its creator. If the gargoyle showed up again, it might be dangerous if Paris wasn't there to call him off.

"So, you really can carry all of us across the Bewilder Forest, the lavender fields, a ton of sunflowers, the lava beds, and the juniper forest?" Paris asked Lunis, wondering where they sat on the back of the dragon. It wasn't like there were any airplane seats. Not that legroom seemed to be a problem. She didn't know how to hold on or where to sit when the blue dragon took off.

"Three ladies riding on my back won't be a problem," Lunis answered. "I've carried magitech equipment that weighs a ton, so I'm certain I can rise to the challenge and carry you all."

Sophia rolled her eyes. "We don't weigh a ton altogether."

The dragon snickered. "I might've had a Dorito dinner last night, but someone had a cheesecake dinner."

Not missing a beat, Sophia laughed. "Here I thought I could veg on the sofa and Netflix without anyone being the wiser."

"I'm always in your head, Soph."

"Apparently," Sophia muttered dryly before turning to Paris. "Don't worry. I'll spell some saddles that will hold you and Willow in place. It won't be a normal ride, but it will be safe. I do apologize in advance for the bad jokes from the dragon. They will be plentiful and probably make you want to throw yourself overboard. If I could make them stop, I would."

Paris giggled, looking forward to the strange mission. The idea was to take Willow to the vortex door that led to Loose Teeth College to negotiate with Headmistress Sham, hopefully ending the feud causing the fairy godmothers so many problems. However, there was a strange, hopeful fluttering in Paris' chest that made her think there was something else unexpected on the horizon of this adventure.

She thought that maybe her more practical side should be on guard, but instead, Paris seemed to want to bound forward, embracing the unknown events that would surely have her adrenal gland racing very soon.

CHAPTER TWENTY-TWO

Headmistress Willow seemed to share Paris' same uncertainty about riding on a dragon when she approached from Happily Ever After mansion. She appeared to be working to keep her expression neutral, although the nervousness was evident in her gaze.

"Is this safe?" Willow asked, eyeing the seats that Sophia had spelled and strapped on the enormous back of the blue dragon. There was plenty of space for three full-grown women, but the seating was still a bit awkward, one would have to admit.

"Not if you don't pay full attention to the safety briefing," Lunis began as Sophia stepped up on the dragon's extended wing and turned, helping Paris onto his back. "If you're seated next to an emergency exit, please read the special instructions card located by your seat very carefully. If you think that, in case of an emergency, you may not be able to perform the described functions, please tell a flight attendant."

Paris slid into the saddle-like seat behind Sophia's and directly beside Willow's and felt around for a safety belt. "Ummmm...aren't all of the seats next to an emergency exit?"

"As you can see," Sophia began, helping Willow onto the dragon's back. "There are no special instruction cards or flight attendants."

"We remind you that this is a non-smoking flight," Lunis continued, ignoring them. "Smoking is prohibited on the plane and at the airport except in the designated areas. Smoking in the lavatories is prohibited. Damaging the smoke detectors is prohibited by law."

Turning to see only the dragon's spiky tail, Paris laughed. "Are there lavatories on board?"

"Please make sure your seat is vertical, your table is folded and locked, and that your seat belt is fastened," Lunis went on in a clerical voice. "Please ensure that your portable electronic devices are on airplane mode until we announce that they're safe to use again."

Glancing at Willow, who wasn't hiding her apprehension, Paris offered a caring smile. "I have so many questions."

Willow nodded, holding the feather quill tightly in her hand that was her magical instrument for directing her magic. "Yes, me too."

"Flight attendants and cabin crew," Lunis said as Sophia slid into her saddle at the front and took the reins. "Please prepare for gate closure, sit, and fasten your seatbelts for takeoff."

Sophia glanced over her shoulder with a wide smile. "Try and enjoy the ride. I'll get us there safely. Lunis will get us there annoyed."

CHAPTER TWENTY-THREE

The wind rushed through Paris' hair as they rose higher into the air. The takeoff on the blue dragon hadn't been as crazy as she would've thought. Not having been on an actual airplane before, Paris didn't have anything to compare it to.

However, she didn't think that one's stomach jumped into one's throat when a plane launched into the air. Nevertheless, once Lunis' feet were off the ground and his wings beating rhythmically, the nervous sensation evaporated at once, completely replaced by awe and anticipation of what lay up ahead.

It was Aunt Sophia's excitement that initially made the tension disappear. As soon as they were high enough to see over the trees of the Bewilder Forest, she let out a shout of surprise.

"Wow, it's so beautiful!" Sophia exclaimed. "I can't believe you created all of this, Pare."

"It's incredibly enchanting," Willow added, looking out at the tops of the many different trees that sprinkled through the Bewilder Forest, the canopy growing thicker as they progressed.

The woods were full of colors and odd twinkling lights. The sounds of strange birds or creatures filtered up from below, audible over the *whooshing* of the dragon's wings.

"Here's a thought…" Lunis began, his voice echoing over the rush of air.

"Get ready for it…" Sophia sighed and looked back over her shoulder at the two women.

"If a tree falls in the forest and no one is around to hear it—"

"Are you wondering if it's heard?" Willow interrupted the dragon.

He shook his head. "No, then I think that my illegal logging business is a success."

Sophia groaned. "I promised you safety. And warned about the bad jokes."

"You weren't kidding." Paris snickered.

Ahead of them at the edge of the Bewilder Forest, something large soared up from the trees. Paris felt the dragon tense under them. She did too. A moment later, she recognized the distinct outline of the gargoyle, its ashen skin like that of stone. However, it didn't fly like a statue, stiff and stoically. Instead, it moved with elegant grace, cutting through the air and seeming to enjoy the flight.

"What's that?" Lunis asked. "Should I fire now and ask more questions later?"

"That's Magnus," Paris answered. "Or as Faraday prefers to call him, it's George. He should be harmless. He's the forest gargoyle."

"I want a gargoyle," Lunis related.

"You don't take care of the hedgehog I got you," Sophia spat. "You're not getting a gargoyle. I wouldn't know how to get one. I didn't think they were real."

"They aren't," Willow explained. "They're another anomaly of Paris' blood manifesting the Bewilder Forest."

"He appears to be showing off for us." Sophia sounded amused.

Paris realized she was right as Magnus glided up and dove again, curving up at the last moment to avoid colliding with the trees. When he rose into the air, his chest up and facing them and his wings beating in their direction, she noticed his gaze intently on her.

She waved at the gargoyle, and he nodded once before diving again and disappearing into the forest, making the branches cave and break from his dramatic exit.

"Well, that was cool," Sophia stated in a rush of excitement.

"It was definitely a unique experience," Willow added, not sounding as entertained, but relief flooding her face when the gargoyle was out of sight.

"I wonder what other cool things your magical forest will show us," Sophia said to Paris over her shoulder.

"I once knew a lumberjack who went into a magical forest," Lunis stated.

"No, you didn't," Sophia interjected.

"When he got there," the blue dragon continued, "he started to swing at a tree, but it suddenly shouted, 'Wait, I'm a talking tree!' My friend, the lumberjack, laughed and said, 'And you will dialogue.'"

Sophia hung her head, seemingly defeated. "Wow, that was particularly bad, Lun. Do you think the magic of the Bewilder Forest is making your jokes worse?"

"I think it's making them better," he answered. "Unfortunately for you, it appears that we're leaving the woods behind... so new scenery means new jokes."

"I can't wait," Sophia muttered, not sounding like she meant it.

Paris peeked forward, catching a view of the lavender fields that lay ahead, smelling their sweet floral aroma as she caught sight of them. Now that they'd made it over the Bewilder Forest, the real work would begin. Without the halfling, they would fly around for miles, never finding the vortex door. It was up to Paris to lead the way so Headmistress Willow could enter Loose Teeth College. Then Paris had other plans she was waiting to unveil—hoping they would help end the battles between the fairies...for good.

CHAPTER TWENTY-FOUR

"Hey, GPS-Girl." Lunis looked back at Paris.

"You want directions," she guessed.

"Yeah, I can cross the lavender fields, veer off to a dark forest unlike the one we came from, or I can go right over a lake," the dragon explained.

Paris blinked ahead, only seeing the lavender field ahead. "Wow, I don't see the last two."

"Well, for one," Sophia began. "The chi of the dragon makes it so we have enhanced vision."

"I thought my demon blood did too," Paris related.

Sophia nodded. "It does, but it's not as strong as our abilities."

"Also," Willow cut in, "you're on a mission to find the vortex door. Since this is your land, it's going to direct your path. I had an inkling it would work that way, but this confirms it, which is exactly one of the main reasons we needed you here."

"And also to keep the gargoyle from causing trouble," Sophia joked.

"Okay, so you're going to cross the lavender fields," Paris stated.

"Stay the course, it is." Lunis flapped his wings, progressing over the beginning of the purple land dotted with rows and rows of lavender.

"After that, we'll cross—"

"Surprise me," Lunis interrupted. "Also, I'd like to enjoy this flight. It's not every day that I get to fly over a field full of my favorite scent."

"Oh, you like lavender?" Willow tried to relax by making conversation. "It's one of my favorites too."

"Yeah, if I had to smell two things for the rest of my life, it would be lavender and citrus," Lunis stated quite seriously. "But that's my two scents."

"Oh, for the love of the angels," Sophia muttered, holding the reins steady and looking over her shoulder at Paris. "Please tell me that he can't come up with jokes for the next land we're crossing."

"Lava," Paris mouthed.

This brought a look of disappointment to her aunt's face. "Yeah, get ready for some bad ones."

"Okay, Siri," Lunis cut in. "Which way? I see beautiful gardens up ahead, a delicious grove of avocado trees, and some lava pits. Which course do I take?"

"Unfortunately, no flowers and guacamole for us," Paris answered. "We need to cross the lava."

"That's okay. I've had my fill of chips and guacamole after last night's Dorito dinner," Lunis stated. "Did you know that you can eat lava?"

"Really?" Willow replied. "I didn't know that."

"Well, only once though," Lunis retorted with a loud laugh as they crossed between the rolling lavender fields and into the hills full of sunflowers.

The entire group was so enamored by the sight of yellow, happy flowers that no one said a word. Even Lunis seemed speechless by the beauty, not making a single joke about sunflowers.

Soon they'd crossed into the land covered in thick pools of bubbling hot lava. The heat rose from the pits of magma, making Paris' cheeks warm instantly. Sweat beaded on Willow's face, and Sophia pulled her long hair up into a high bun on her head in a swift movement. The only one who didn't seem to mind the hot lava lands was Lunis, who was singing *Everyday is a Winding Road* by Sheryl Crow.

"Your dragon is so strange," Paris remarked as she pulled off her leather jacket and fastened it around her waist.

"You have no idea," Sophia stated.

"This is the place to play 'the floor is lava' game," Lunis sang, swaying from side to side like he was dancing.

"I think I'd rather not, please." Willow held onto her saddle for dear life, her face now covered in sweat.

"Fine." Lunis sighed. "Okay, but you know who lost 'the floor is lava' game the worst?"

"Who?" Willow asked because she didn't know it was a setup.

"Everyone in Pompeii 79 A.D."

"Wow, that one was in particularly bad form." Sophia shook her head at her dragon.

The blue dragon shrugged. "Hey, I don't promise that the jokes won't be offensive."

"Or funny," the dragonrider added.

"Hey, Google Maps," Lunis called to Paris. "Do I turn right at the Starbucks? Go left to the ice land? Or continue straight to the juniper forest?"

"There's a Starbucks?" Sophia asked, perking up.

"Well, it looks like a knockoff," Lunis stated. "It's called Strawbucks."

"Your blood is very interesting." Willow gave Paris a curious look.

Paris nodded. "Although I could use an iced latte, we're headed to the center of the juniper forest."

"Oh, good," Sophia said with a sigh. "There's no possible way this jokester has one for junipers."

"Juniper?" Lunis asked. "I thought you hardly knew her."

"Nope," Sophia said at once, adamantly shaking her head. "That one doesn't work."

"Oh, come on, Soph," he argued. "Did-ja-nip-her? Get it…"

"Try again, Lun."

"Knock, knock," the blue dragon said as they crossed out of the lava pits. The air automatically cooled, giving them all some relief.

"Who's there?" Paris asked, unable to resist.

"Juniper," he answered.

"Juniper who?" Willow asked.

"Juniper her in the butt." Lunis laughed, and they all joined him as the blue dragon soared over the twisted trees and red hills, headed for the vortex door up ahead.

CHAPTER TWENTY-FIVE

"You really did find it," Willow said in an astonished voice as they landed near the vortex door as if she didn't at first believe that Paris had found it. Maybe she was holding out hope although not wanting to get her hopes up, Paris reasoned.

As Paris had remembered, the vortex doors were in a large set of stones lined up in the sand with an "X" in the center that created four quadrants. It was known as a medicine wheel.

"Do you know how it works?" Sophia asked once Lunis was on the ground.

Paris nodded. "Yes, one quadrant takes you here, the second to Loose Teeth College, the third to the magical carnival, and the fourth apparently to the Seelie court."

"But you know which one is which, right?" Sophia helped Willow down, although Paris jumped down on her own.

Paris pointed at the far left quadrant. "That one is to the carnival."

"That's where I'm going," Lunis chimed.

"Yeah, no, you're not, Tubs," Sophia stated. "You can't fit in that medicine wheel without messing it up."

The blue dragon huffed. "Oh, then I guess I'm the Uber, and you're leaving me behind."

"We're staying back," Sophia answered. "We'll wait for you two to return."

"It's only me going to Loose Teeth College." Willow pointed at the quadrant on the top right. "It's that one there."

"I don't think that's a good idea," Paris argued. "The tooth fairies have proven that they're on the attack. Even though you're going on a peace mission, those three students behind things might not care. I suspect they really couldn't care less. If they spot you, they might attack. You're on their territory."

Willow smiled politely. "I'm sure I'll be fine. Although Headmistress Sham and I haven't seen eye-to-eye, we've always tried to be civil. She wouldn't condone her students endangering me."

"Yes, but she doesn't seem to have control," Paris stated. "She wants things to be civil so she can get funding from the Seelie court once more. It's obvious her students are creating all the problems."

"So the Seelie court are fairies?" Sophia asked. "But they're different than you all?"

"We're like a sub-race," Willow answered. "They're the original clan and have stayed hidden and remote since the beginning. Some split from them early on, but the founding fairies are who makes them up. Their magic is much stronger than other fairies. Our history is very complicated."

"Try having all your ancestors in your head," Lunis related.

"That's the way to the Seelie Court?" Sophia pointed at the other quadrant.

"Yes," Willow affirmed. "But we're not allowed in there as long as the feud wages on, which I fear means that we'll always remain split."

"Which is only creating problems for everyone," Paris added.

"Well, I think that Pare is right. She should accompany you," Sophia said to Willow. "I know that you're very capable of negotiating and trying to find a peaceful solution. But Paris knows combat magic and has other skills that might come in handy. It's better to be safe rather than sorry. It sounds like you can't trust these tooth fairies."

Willow considered this for a moment, indecision on her face. Finally, she nodded and squared her shoulders. "Okay, fine. I'll have you accompany me. We're going to avoid confrontation at all costs. I'm here to talk. Hopefully, we can make progress that benefits all… however, as long as the tooth fairies are supplying the Fang Wellspring with dark magic, I fear there will continue to be tension between us."

Paris followed Willow to the quadrant that led to Loose Teeth College, her eyes skipping to the one next to it that went to the Seelie Court. "Well, maybe there's a way to create a solution that works for everyone."

CHAPTER TWENTY-SIX

Cold air and a swamp smell accosted Paris' senses when the vortex door transported her to Loose Teeth College. Compared to Happily Ever After College, the grounds for the tooth fairies were dark although Paris had thought it was daytime.

Headmistress Willow must have sensed Paris' confusion because she nodded, giving her a commiserating look. "It's always nighttime here at Loose Teeth College. And it's always fall."

The fairy godmother tightened her blue gown around her neck, shivering from the chilly autumn wind as leaves swept through the air on the breeze.

"Why?" Paris asked, then thought the answer should be obvious. The tooth fairies were the opposite of the fairy godmothers. They liked chaos and worked at night, stealing teeth from children, giving them disappearing money in return. The fairy godmothers conversely brought love and enjoyed things related to spring-like growth, abundance, and rebirth.

"Because when we were assigned our roles, a set of fairies to create love and one to create power," Willow explained, "the decision was that we'd be opposites so we didn't pull from the same resources. The tooth fairies pulled on the night and fall and had instructions to create a well of magical power. We received the spring and daylight, although it can be night at the college because we enjoy balance. Our job was to increase love so we took our different roles."

"The two colleges were placed in the same bubble to protect them and share resources and power, right?" Paris asked, remembering what Willow had told her about the conception of the fairy organizations.

"Yes, along with the Seelie Court," Willow answered. "As the oldest group of fairies—the originals—they have a huge store of power that helps to keep us hidden. Without them, we would be discoverable and vulnerable. Our grounds would be subject to outside influences. Having the perfect balance of spring and love would be impossible."

"The queen, Helena MacGillie, wanted the tooth fairies and the fairy godmothers to get along, right?" Paris' eyes adjusted to the dark grounds of Loose Teeth College. "Why would she care?"

"Harmony is the cardinal rule of the Seelie Court." Willow's look of regret was evident on her face even in the shadows cast by a narrow nearby structure. "But it goes deeper than that. You see, her history influences Queen Helena MacGillie. The Seelie Court and the Unseelie Court, much like the fairy godmothers and the tooth fairies, are opposites.

"One represents winters and autumn and malice, while the other is associated with spring and summer and happiness. Both courts reside inside the vortex door, but only one is truly recognized right now because the Seelie queen currently reigns supreme. I think Queen Helena MacGillie's divide from the Unseelie is one reason she dislikes so much that we don't get along."

Willow paused, looking around the quiet grounds. They appeared to be on the outskirts of a winter forest since most of the trees had lost their leaves. After a moment, she shrugged. "There are always battles waged between the Unseelie and Seelie. There has been since the beginning. That's why many regard us and the fae as 'solitaries' because our ancestors split from them, not wanting to be a part of the tension and fighting any longer."

"So Queen Helena MacGillie is mad that the fairy godmothers and the tooth fairies don't get along because her people don't get along with the Unseelie?" Paris asked, confused by the irony but also understanding it.

"The structure between the fairy courts has always been political," Willow explained. "Queen Helena MacGillie is motivated by that, which has affected her people for as long as history. She can't endorse our divide with the tooth fairies because the wars with the Unseelie have created so many problems through the centuries. Yet, it's a result of both courts being unwilling to strike a balance and compromise."

"Seems a bit hypocritical," Paris remarked, a chill running down her back at the sound of an owl hooting ominously in the distance.

"As I said, it's political," Willow stated. "Queen Helena MacGillie has always presented herself as a peacemaker, yet the battles continue between her court and the Unseelie. What you have to remember is that both Seelie and Unseelie are exceptionally deceptive. What you see is definitely not what you get. What they say isn't what they mean. Again, this is another reason that many of our ancestors left the court long ago."

"So she's never tried to fix the actual problems, has she?" Paris asked.

Willow pursed her lips, thinking. "There are centuries of stubbornness that are hard to erase. I believe that both sides think they're trying but are unwilling to budge. I guess I can understand because although negotiations have spanned the years, no progress has happened. After all, compromises often mean that someone loses."

This notion assaulted Paris, but it rang so true. Usually, a compromise meant that both parties gave something up. It sounded like the Seelie and Unseelie were unwilling to give an inch. They didn't seem so different from the tooth fairies and fairy godmothers in that regard. Both were remaining stubbornly in place and battling each other over feuds that seemingly they could easily erase.

They needed new solutions, Paris thought. *They needed an outsider who thought differently...*

CHAPTER TWENTY-SEVEN

Paris and Headmistress Starr had only taken a few steps away from the row of trees when they both froze. The narrow structures around them came into view, shining in the moonlight illuminating them.

They were in a cemetery.

Eerie wasn't the right word for the cluster of tombstones sprinkled between them and the large gothic mansion in the distance. It felt like the vortex door had dropped Paris into a horror movie, and the deranged murderer was loose in the haunted woods behind them, racing in their direction.

She took a step forward and caught a thick cobweb in the mouth. Reeling back, Paris swiped her hands over her face as a black bat swooped down at her head while screeching. She dropped to her knees and suddenly felt a resounding evil nearby.

Immediately, she knew that her demon blood was picking up on something evil close around them. However, the possibilities of what it could be were endless. They were in a cemetery, at a college for mean fairies who created dark magic. And bats were attacking her head and cobwebs assaulting her face.

All of that had been in the last several moments.

Daring to pull her hands away from her face, Paris righted herself, scanning the area for more dive-bombing bats, hoping there was nothing more sinister about them.

"We need to hurry to the mansion," Willow whispered, pointing at the dark building lurking in the distance. It had the opposite vibe as the Happily Ever After College mansion, which felt like grandma's house. The three-story house looked like a creepy haunted mansion with shadows moving in the candle-lit windows. Its roof shingles were broken and missing in several places.

The exterior was in horrible disrepair, with many of the windows boarded up. Although Paris could see much of the gothic architecture detail, darkness covered it, as if ghosts around it were casting it in weird shadows.

"Why do we need to hurry?" Paris dared to ask and again realized that the answer was obvious. They were in a cemetery, being attacked by flying pests and shivering in the chilly cold of the grounds.

"I think you were right to accompany me." Willow moved close to Paris. "Someone is watching us, and I fear they will soon attack. We need to get up to the mansion before it's too late. It's not safe out here in the open."

Paris scanned the grounds suddenly even more on alert, her demon blood homing in on the potential dangers. Immediately she caught sight of two figures on the opposite side of the cemetery. She tensed as a loud cackle filled the air. A sharp *whizzing* followed as something shot in their direction.

Without hesitation, Paris grabbed the headmistress by the hand and hauled her forward toward the mansion.

CHAPTER TWENTY-EIGHT

S mall fireballs whizzed by them less than a few seconds after Paris and Willow started running. Fireballs were gnome magic. The gnomes had gifted Paris' mother that skill. Aunt Sophia had it because of the chi of the dragon. Paris' father had it because of his demon blood.

That meant although Paris hadn't attempted to shoot any, she probably could. What she was sure of was that regular fairies shouldn't have fireball magic—not unless they were using dark magic.

The realization immediately made Paris tense. Not only was she on the evil tooth fairies' territory, but they had weapons they shouldn't and they weren't going to play fair. Paris remembered her run-in with Courtney Montgomery at the magical carnival. The fairy had fought dirty, using the mirrors in the fun house to try and confuse Paris. Now Courtney's wand was broken. However, as a fireball rushed by Paris' head, nearly singeing her hair, she realized that one of the other Knees probably had their wand full of dark magic.

Grabbing Willow by the arm, Paris pushed her around a tall head-stone, unfortunately knocking her back into it harder than she would've liked.

"Sorry," Paris whispered, taking in the shocked expression on the soft and dainty fairy godmother's face. She wasn't used to battle or danger or being outside her cozy grounds.

Willow Starr definitely wasn't used to being shot at with deadly fireballs.

Glancing out around the large tombstone of a cross, Paris tried to make out where the one was throwing the fireballs. She'd only seen two. She caught sight of one figure straight ahead, standing on top of a squatly mausoleum with a pitched roof. It was Courtney Montgomery, her high pigtails making the shape of her head distinct with the moonlight filtering through the trees behind her.

Willow and Mae Ling had said that without a wand, a fairy from Loose Teeth College couldn't pull and use magic from the Fang Wellspring. This meant that Courtney had a new wand, which was unlikely since they were only issued one, or the attacker was somewhere else.

Just in time, but not nearly as fast as she would've liked, Paris saw a pale face peek out from behind a statue of an angel on top of a tomb. She pointed her wand, and immediately Paris reacted.

"Duck," Paris encouraged Willow, jumping up and covering the fairy godmother's head with her arms and pushing her to the ground. Not a second later, three consecutive fireballs blasted the tombstone. Their embers sprayed out around it, catching fire on Willow's billowing gown.

Immediately, Paris slapped at the potential fire but didn't waste much of their precious time on the task. The tooth fairies knew their position, which was a bad thing. Paris had the job of protecting Willow Starr, which made things more complicated.

The mansion where they needed to get to was far on the other side of the creepy cemetery. Even worse, Paris didn't have high hopes that when they reached the haunted house, their jobs would get any easier. Maybe it had been a mistake to come here to try and negotiate peace. However, she had signed on to help, and help was what she'd do.

Pulling Willow up from her crouched position, Paris gave her a sturdy look and spoke in a rush. "When I say go, you're going to run for the mansion—"

"But—" Willow tried to interrupt, fear heavy in her large eyes.

Paris shook her head. "Just do it. I'll cover your back."

"But you'll be left behind with them…"

"Don't worry about me," Paris encouraged. "My demon blood will ensure I'll catch up in no time. First I have to teach some jerks a lesson."

Willow nodded, not looking confident.

The sounds of approaching footsteps made Paris realize that their brief moment to strategize was over. It was time to move and fight.

She hauled Willow upright. "Pull up that gown and run like hell."

Maybe the headmistress was offended by her curse word. Whatever her reason, she remained frozen—unmoving.

"Go," Paris urged, nearly pushing the fairy godmother toward the house as another loud cackle filled the cold night air.

CHAPTER TWENTY-NINE

S pinning on the spot, Paris popped out from her spot behind the tombstone, taking two risks simultaneously. The first was exposing herself briefly, deciding that she needed to be on the move to maximize her advantages when facing two opponents at once. The second was that for the first time, she attempted to shoot a fireball.

Trying a complicated spell for the first time was much harder in the heat of battle, with adrenaline rushing. However, Paris also believed in trial by fire. She laughed at her bad pun as she extended her finger and aimed it straight toward the angel statue in the distance as she ran for cover behind another headstone.

This one was more solid than the cross that she and Willow had stationed themselves behind, providing a bit more coverage. That was about as much good fortune as Paris had right then since no fireball had soared toward the evil fairy.

Encouraged by her movement, a series of fireballs hit the thick tombstone, issuing sparks into the air overhead. Paris ducked, but she didn't have to worry about the embers like before with Willow.

Speaking of the fairy godmother, Paris spied her darting between headstones up ahead—her pale blue gown making her presence hard not to notice. A fireball soared past where Paris was stationed and nearly hit Willow as she ran for the mansion.

"Watch out!" Paris yelled.

The head mistress jerked her head over her shoulder. Seeing the fireball soaring in her direction, she held up her feather quill, sending a spell in its direction. Several rose petals appeared in the air and swept toward it on a soft blanket of wind.

What happened next would've been comical if it wasn't happening to someone that Paris cared about. The flower petals collided with the fireball, making it pause. At first, Paris thought the spell would work, knocking the attack to the ground and keeping it from hitting Willow.

In seemingly slow motion, the rose petals swept forward as the fireball rolled in place in the air. Then in a rush, the petals flew toward it and were instantly charred to ash. The fireball, seemingly encouraged by that, spun in the air like a car about to take off and shot forward—straight for the fairy godmother.

CHAPTER THIRTY

Paris threw up her hand, ready to throw a combat spell at the fireball to defend Willow. Thankfully she didn't have to because the fairy godmother used a simple, tried-and-true technique. The headmistress dropped to her front, her face and everything else planting straight into the cemetery's mud.

The fireball soared over her head and hit another tombstone, exploding a safe distance away.

Letting out a breath, Paris watched as Willow crawled to safety behind another stone, her face and front covered in thick, dark mud. This was exactly why fairy godmothers weren't cut out for battle. They didn't have the instinct or knowledge to defend themselves. They didn't know how to go on the offensive, which was Paris' next goal.

She turned her attention back to where the two evil fairies were stationed somewhere on the other side of the cemetery. Pulling in a deep breath, Paris prepared herself for another attempt at creating a fireball. She knew she couldn't overthink it. Desire was the biggest part of a spell. Know-how usually came later.

Using the motivation in her chest, Paris peeked out briefly from behind her shield and pointed her finger at the angel tombstone where she could make out a part of a figure.

Something shot from her finger this time. Unfortunately, what it was wouldn't light dry kindling on fire. A single spark shot through the air, but the wind immediately extinguished it.

"Oh, and they think you're so great, halfling," Courtney Montgomery's voice issued from her place standing on top of the mausoleum to the far left. She stood on the roof, her hands on her hips and her pigtails blowing in the wind. Like the first time that Paris had the unfortunate experience of meeting Becky's sister, she was wearing the awful black tutu like she was some gothic ballerina.

Paris also remembered from her prior encounter with Courtney that she liked to talk a big game and was easy to goad. That was a key strategy for taking down opponents in Paris' book. Get them riled up, and they wouldn't know what hit them when attacked. Literally and figuratively.

"You can't shoot a fireball," Courtney continued from her place up high.

"What can you do with your broken wand?" Paris yelled, putting herself squarely behind the tombstone as she heard footsteps to the right. The other fairy was on the move.

"Shut your mouth!" Courtney exclaimed.

"Okay, then we won't talk about how your mother cut you off from your family money," Paris taunted.

"You will pay for exposing me!"

"We'll see, Miss Wand-Less."

Paris ran through her other combat options. Wind was her best bet as a half-magician since that was the element they controlled. She could use it to knock Courtney to the ground, but that might break a bone or two. She reasoned that Courtney wasn't the threat. She was an annoyance. Paris needed to keep her attention on the one sending fireballs.

The sound of footsteps paused.

Paris peeked over her shield. Her evil compass told her that the fairy was a little closer and hiding behind a narrow tree trunk. That could be perfect for a fire attack—if only Paris could launch one.

"Why exactly are you rejects attacking Happily Ever After College and fairy godmothers again?" Paris asked, buying some time as she tried to work out how the fireball spell should work. It would involve elemental magic, but if she was pulling from her demon blood, she could rely on something else—something more primitive...like hot, boiling anger.

"Because you all deserve it!" Courtney replied, her voice shrill.

The rustling near the tree sounded again. Paris could only assume that the other fairy was buying time too. She'd probably used up a lot of magic with her other fireballs and was waiting for the Fang Wellspring power to store up again. However, Paris remembered what she'd heard about the dark magic. It was unpredictable. It could burn a person up. It was also uncontrollable. If this fight went on too long, Paris might not be fighting simple fireballs. It could be explosions and walls of fire.

It was time to put her theory on the fireballs to the test and send these fairies running so Willow could do her job and try to negotiate for peace.

"We deserve it!" Paris screamed, her voice aching in her throat, thinking how the evil fairies had invaded the Enchanted Grounds and destroyed the Serenity Gardens and Observatory. How they'd tried to hurt Willow earlier. How they were storing up dark magic that furthered the problems of the world. The last part was what made Paris the angriest.

Feeling her hot emotions build inside her, Paris spun out from behind her hiding place, not worried about being exposed. With brand-new confidence, Paris held up her hand and shot a spell straight at the winter tree.

What happened next nearly blew Paris off her feet and did blow her mind with astonishment.

CHAPTER THIRTY-ONE

A blast of fire, hot and powerful, shot from Paris' hand. The force as it soared in the opposite direction was almost enough to knock her backward, but she braced herself.

The orange and red fire was so bright up close that it blinded Paris momentarily. She turned her head to the side, and with an unseen force, she directed the fireball toward the tree. It was like leading something with a leash that connected to her thoughts. She instinctively knew she could send it almost anywhere she desired, rather than shoot it in one path and watch it follow a trajectory.

The idea that she'd produced a fireball from nowhere was astonishing. However, Paris didn't take too long to enjoy her brief success. Instead, she watched as the ball of fire hit the tree, blasting the trunk and sending flames into the dry branches—engulfing it in a blaze.

From behind it, a woman screamed and immediately jumped back to avoid getting burned. The light of the flames was so bright that it was hard to make out much besides her outline. All Paris could see was the wand she held and that she had short hair or had pulled it back.

The fairy didn't stand behind the fire long either. Realizing that she was overmatched and probably low on magic stores, the evil tooth fairy turned and ran in the opposite direction for the woods behind the cemetery.

"Don't leave me!" Courtney yelled to her friend.

Deciding that she needed a little help down, Paris lifted her hand and shot a neat bit of wind at the woman standing on top of the short mausoleum. She didn't feel the least bit bad when Courtney was swept off the roof and tumbled to the ground, landing in a thick pile of leaves—rolling over several times very ungracefully.

She jumped to her feet rather clumsily and glared at Paris, the bright fire licking at the tree making the glare on her face more than apparent. However, when something rustled at Paris' back, Courtney Montgomery spun around and fled, taking the same path as her troublemaker friend.

CHAPTER THIRTY-TWO

On hyper-alert, Paris spun around, ready to launch another attack. She relaxed at the sight of Willow Starr, who was almost unrecognizable. Mud covered the fairy godmother from head to toe. The blue of her gown wasn't visible under the thick clumps of dirt. Worse, caked-on mud masked the usually light expression on the headmistress' face.

However, the expression of concern was still evident in the sweet fairy godmother's face as she looked Paris over. "Are you okay?"

She nodded, glancing over her shoulder to ensure that there weren't any more attackers on the way. Hadn't Willow said that the Knees were known as three troublemaker rebel fairies? Courtney, Sidney, and Whitney. There had only been two there in the cemetery...unless one was hiding.

"I'm fine." Paris listened for the sound of another attack. There didn't appear to be anyone else by the looks of it. All she could hear was the crackling of the fire as the tree in the cemetery burned. "Are you?"

Willow stepped forward, holding up her hand with the feather quill. "I'll be okay and clean myself up, but first things first."

A moment later, a stream of water shot from the quill and doused the tree, doing an incredibly efficient job of extinguishing the fire.

"Well, that was impressive magic on your part," Willow said with a relieved sigh, turning to Paris. "I knew you had diverse talents based on your genetics, but I had no idea you could produce fireballs."

"I didn't either," Paris admitted. "That fairy. She shouldn't have been able to, should she?"

Willow nodded and pointed the feather quill at herself. A moment later, all the mud disappeared from her gown, hair, and face, making her look normal and elegant once more. "Yes, the Fang Wellspring makes much impossible magic possible for those who use it. That wouldn't be a problem, but most who do pull from it have nefarious intentions. The wrong magic is always dangerous in the wrong hands."

"Which is the main reason you won't condone what the tooth fairies do," Paris guessed.

"I can't," Willow stated. "It undoes the good work that we aim to accomplish as fairy godmothers. Even if it keeps things divided, as long as the tooth fairies supply dark magic, there can be no true truce between us. However, let's hope that although we won't mend fences that we can at least agree to stay out of each other's territory. At this point, I only want the tooth fairies to leave us alone."

Paris nodded, although she had another idea in mind. It might not work. She had no evidence telling her that it ever would. But she thought it was possibly worth a try depending on how the meeting went with Headmistress Sham.

"Well, I think we're safe to proceed to the main building now." Willow looked around in her usual dignified manner. The grounds of Loose Teeth College were quiet now, save for the rusting of the leafless branches as the winds rocked through them.

"Yeah, but didn't you say there were three rebel fairies who had a grudge against us?" Paris questioned, still on high alert.

"I did. Although I suspect they're the boldest who are willing to attack. Maybe one of the others gave up or was dissuaded by what happened when Courtney lost her wand. What they're doing by outwardly going after us and specifically you is dangerous. I think back there, you proved you're a force that they better think twice about messing with, even when they outnumber you. I think the third one must've fled."

Paris nodded, although she wasn't so sure. "Yeah, let's hope that all served as a warning to them. Maybe their attempts at sabotaging us are already over, and peace talks with Headmistress Sham will be easy."

Willow let out an unsettled breath. "I'm usually one to be optimistic, but discussions with Headmistress Sham have never gone well. We've never been able to see eye-to-eye. It's almost like we speak a different language."

"Well, fairy godmothers and tooth fairies are very different," Paris reasoned.

"That we are." Willow set off for the large, dark mansion. "My time away from them made me underestimate the fairies. I'm grateful that you insisted on accompanying me, Paris. If you hadn't, I fear I might not have survived those attacks."

Paris shuddered. "Then we wouldn't be having a simple peace negotiation. There would be an all-out war."

CHAPTER THIRTY-THREE

Paris could understand why the tooth fairies would be cross about losing funding from the Seelie queen, Helena MacGillie. Their headquarters at Loose Teeth College was close to looking condemned.

The mansion was about the size of where she lived at Happily Ever After College, but the similarities stopped there. From the other side of the cemetery, Paris hadn't noticed that many of the shutters were hanging off their hinges beside the numerous windows. The gray and black paint was peeling off most of the exterior, which was crooked and falling off in places. Crows filled the many spires and peered down at Paris and Willow when they approached.

Maybe back in its time, the mansion was nice with its Victorian character and many angles. However, presently, the building seemed to have taken on the vibe of its corrupt residents, as many homes do. It felt creepy and conniving and full of darkness—both in the literal and figurative sense.

The fog that slinked along the edges of the large grounds seemed like it was serving as a welcoming committee when Paris and Willow made their way up the broken stairs to the entrance. Paris half-expected a refined magitech AI butler similar to Wilfred Biltmore to answer the door and greet them. Instead, the front door flung back as they approached, showing a dark entryway full of a dank aroma.

Without hesitating, Willow picked up her blue gown and stepped over the threshold, entering the mansion.

"Is it safe to walk in?" Paris paused in front of the door and peered at the cloudy windows along the side of the house. Firelight flickered on the other side.

"No," Willow answered. "Many won't approve of our presence here. However, Headmistress Sham knows we're here, or she wouldn't have opened the door for us. So she wants us here."

"Oh." Paris hurried to catch up with Willow as she progressed into the house. Whereas Happily Ever After was full of color and warmth, this place was a palette of muted tones and chilly to the bone. Even though Paris saw a fire burning at the far end of the large entryway beside a tall staircase, its warmth didn't radiate through the space.

Shelves lined the wall at the back, but they were empty of books or artifacts. The rug under her boots was burned in places and ragged with wear in others. The chandelier flickered overhead like it was considering burning out entirely or a poltergeist operated it.

Unlike the fairy godmother mansion, there wasn't a long hallway that led to the conservatory, dining hall, and other classrooms. The intricate staircase at the front of the house was similar, but that's where the resemblances stopped. Instead, the entryway was a large, cavernous room with stairs that seemed to lead to several different hallways. Other doors were positioned around the entryway, probably leading to more hallways or large rooms. Paris had zero urge to explore this place. All she wanted to do was get in and get out.

"She'll be down here," Willow murmured, taking a right into the first door.

Paris wanted to ask how she was so sure but decided that it wasn't a necessary question. Willow had obviously had many dealings with the headmistress of Loose Teeth College, and it sounded like their history hadn't been a pleasant one. Instead, she followed the fairy godmother, entering a hallway straight out of a horror movie.

"Redrum, anyone," Paris joked, taking in the yellowing wallpaper over the stained wainscoting. The lanterns that flecked the wall weren't all lit, casting much of the long corridor in shadows.

"What's that?" Willow asked, flicking her feathered quill and producing an orb of light to guide them.

"Nothing, just wondering if we're about to be murdered," Paris said.

"Not on my watch," a deep voice echoed from the end of the hallway.

Paris glanced up, not having seen anyone move into the space. She halted, held her breath, and marveled at how the woman on the far side of the corridor was beautiful and hideous at the same time.

CHAPTER THIRTY-FOUR

S tanding in the middle of the darkened hallway was a tall fairy woman with long black hair and a pale white face. She wore a dark red dress that showed her figure, unlike the flowing gowns the fairy godmothers wore. Along her bare arms were several leather belt-like straps with buckles. She wore a black cross around her neck that matched her pointy fingernails and the dark eyeshadow around her eyes. When she swayed back and forth, the various chains fashioned to the large skirt of her dress clanged.

She had a strange allure that made her appear beautiful, almost like Willow, who was poised and wise and had many attractive features. However, there was also something about the woman that put fear into Paris she'd never felt before.

It might've been that standing next to her was a large crow that looked like it was ready to peck Paris' eyes out. It also could have been that in the fairy's hand was a dead bird. She sorely hoped that wasn't their welcoming gift.

"Headmistress Sham." Willow seemed unafraid as she strode down the hallway now with more speed, heading toward the other woman. "I thought you knew we were here."

"Of course," the woman said, her voice deep and gravelly but carrying a strange melodic quality to it. "My crystal ball told me of your arrival as soon as you stepped across the holy grounds."

Willow huffed suddenly, her disapproval apparent. Paris wasn't sure if it was because Headmistress Sham was using a crystal ball to spy on visitors. That method was notorious for being full of dark magic. Possibly it was because she seemed to be inferring that the creepy cemetery where the students attacked them was holy grounds. Still, if she couldn't see them before that, she wouldn't know that her students had ambushed them.

"No, you won't come to harm while you're here," Headmistress Sham said to Paris when she approached on the other side of Willow. "I've been hoping to receive a visit from Headmistress Starr for quite some time since I couldn't find Happily Ever After College after you moved it." She glanced back at the fairy godmother, looking down at her as she was so much taller. "At last, you've returned to mend relations. My students have been told not to harm our visitors."

As she concluded, whispers echoed from behind the various doors along the hallway. Paris glanced back and forth, on the alert. However, the fairy godmother didn't seem unnerved by the eerie sounds emanating behind the closed doors.

Willow pursed her lips. "I'm afraid you misunderstand the nature of my visit. I'm not here to mend things but rather because your students have been doing precisely that—harming us. They've been attacking our students and grounds."

The look of shock spoke of the headmistress' surprise. The way she crushed the dead bird's body in her hand indicated her anger at learning this news. She dropped the dead bird, and the crow squawked and hopped for it at once.

Headmistress Sham spun and hurried down the hallway to a doorway at the end. "Follow me. It sounds as if we have much to discuss."

CHAPTER THIRTY-FIVE

The dark fairy led them into a large office that was the antithesis of Willow's at Happily Ever After College. Like the paint on the mansion's exterior, the wallpaper in Headmistress Sham's office was peeling. The wood molding around the doors, windows, and ceiling was dented and scorched as if several fires had occurred in the office.

Unlike in Headmistress Starr's office, the desk wasn't prominent and the furniture elegant. Instead, there was a small writing desk pushed into a dark corner that was full of cobwebs. A rickety chair that looked close to breaking on its next use sat in front of the unorganized desk piled high with yellowing parchment and old books.

Beside the desk was a small round table with the crystal ball. Purple clouds and shadows filled it. Two other chairs that also didn't look like they could withstand another use surrounded it.

However, Headmistress Sham pointed at the seats with her long, pointed fingernail. "Sit."

Paris wanted to protest that she'd prefer to stand, but the crow that had followed them into the office squawked, hopping into the air. He seemed to be saying, "Do it, or I'll poke your eyes out."

Deciding that she'd rather fall on her butt than lose an eye, Paris cautiously took a seat in the black wicker chair. Thankfully it was stronger than it appeared, holding her weight. Willow did the same, not hesitating as she pulled herself up to the table in a dignified manner. Her eyes flicked to the smoky crystal ball, disapproval heavy in her gaze before she glanced up at Headmistress Sham with a sturdy, unintimidated expression.

The tooth fairy picked up a wand on the side of her desk and pointed it at the door. It shut at once with a loud *slam*.

"We won't be heard now. Tell me exactly what has been going on."

CHAPTER THIRTY-SIX

"Just now, in the cemetery, we were attacked by some of your students," Willow began in an unwavering tone.

"You did trespass onto our grounds," Headmistress Sham countered at once, cutting her off. "You know that many of our students have a rivalry with fairy godmothers."

"A rivalry would be somewhat harmless," Willow argued. "What's happening with your students borders on dangerous."

The dark fairy directed her wand at the chair, and it turned on its own and scooted itself right underneath her. She sat without looking down. Willow rolled her eyes at this as if unimpressed at how lazy the other fairy was for not using physical efforts to do such a simple task.

"I'm certain this is another of your exaggerations, Willow. I'm sure they were only playing with you."

"They threw fireballs at us," Headmistress Starr said in a tone Paris had never heard her use before.

"It was only one of them who could throw fireballs," Paris dared to enter the conversation. "If you've been waiting for Headmistress Starr to enter your grounds, why would you have allowed such treatment?"

The tooth fairy slowly revolved in Paris' direction. "You're Guinevere Paris Beaufont. That's what my crystal ball told me when you entered. A halfling with demon blood. Quite the interesting combinations."

"I go by Paris."

"Well, Paris, I wasn't aware that anyone attacked you, but I've told the students that if the headmistress for Happily Ever After College was to visit, they shouldn't harm her." She shrugged, holding her wand and eyeing it with mock interest. "I mean, if they wanted to play a few mischievous pranks on you, well, I don't see the harm with that."

Willow leaned forward. "Again, they threw fireballs at us. That's not an innocent prank. They were aiming to kill."

"It was only one of them shooting fireballs," Paris stated. "The other one wasn't because it was Courtney Montgomery, and she has a broken wand."

At this, Headmistress Sham seemed unnerved, sitting back. The crow squawked, flying up to the desk, the beating of its wings making loose papers sweep off its surface and fall to the floor.

The tooth fairy looked over her shoulder suddenly, glaring at the crow. "I know that Courtney doesn't have a wand anymore."

The bird cawed once more.

Slowly, deliberately, Headmistress Sham turned back to Paris and Willow. "So you entered my grounds to discuss fixing relations to appease Queen Helena MacGillie, and students attacked you. I apologize. I'll look into the matter later. The crystal ball can't tell me anything that happens in the holy grounds of the college so I'll have to question the students."

"I think it was either Sidney Beater or Whitney Ives," Willow stated. "I've heard for a while that they've been talking horribly about fairy godmothers on Roya Lane and other places. I've reason to believe that they've been planning to attack us for a while."

Headmistress Sham sighed, shaking her head and not taking this seriously. "Oh, come on. Again, you know there's tension between our schools. That's why you're here, to resolve things."

It was Willow's turn to sigh now. "Your inability to hear that which displeases you is as I remember. As I said before, I'm not here to mend relations so that Queen Helena MacGillie reinstates your subsidies."

"But you came here!" Headmistress Sham exclaimed as her face flushed red.

"Yes, because your students attacked the Serenity Garden and Observatory at Happily Ever After College," Willow stated.

The tooth fairy narrowed her eyes. "That's preposterous. We can't locate your stupid grounds since you put the Bewilder Forest in place."

"The Bewilder Forest has changed, and in doing so, it doesn't block tooth fairies from entering," Willow stated. "I believe Courtney Montgomery had inside information that helped her to find it, based on her family's association with Happily Ever After College. I had no idea until recently that she was the sister of a student at my school and the daughter of a fairy godmother. She could easily have gotten enough information from them to locate the vortex door and used dark magic from the Fang Wellspring to negotiate her way through the Bewilder Forest."

This seemed to surprise Headmistress Sham too but also give her a bit of satisfaction. "Oh, well look at that. We got the black sheep of a goody-goody family."

Willow restrained herself with a slow, steadying breath. "I think you're missing the point. Your students have trespassed onto the grounds of Happily Ever After College and twice damaged our property. On a third occasion, Courtney Montgomery was intercepted on her own by Paris. There was a confrontation, and that's when her wand broke."

The tooth fairy spun at once, glaring at Paris. "It was you."

"She attacked me," Paris stated. "And she was trespassing on our grounds to do more damage."

"I'll deal with Courtney then," Headmistress Sham stated. "But it doesn't sound like you have any evidence to prove that others were involved or that this should be directly associated with Loose Teeth College."

"For one," Willow began, "there is no way that only one fairy could've done all the destruction to the Serenity Garden or the Observatory—even one with dark magic. Secondly, they left behind a signature of sorts. On both occasions, they burned a giant tooth into the areas they destroyed."

The crow cawed in response to this, but Headmistress Sham didn't. This wasn't going the way she'd expected. She glanced at the crow, and they seemed to have a silent conversation before she turned her attention back to Headmistress Starr.

"I'm here to ask you to intervene, stopping your students from any further attacks," Willow continued. "I fear that Courtney Montgomery might be particularly ruthless now that she's lost her wand and her trust fund."

"She what?" Headmistress Sham asked at once, shock covering her features.

Willow cleared her throat, the picture of poise in comparison to the other fairy. "The Montgomerys are a very well-endowed family. The children have large trust funds, but Courtney expressed to Paris when they fought that if the world found out a Montgomery was at Loose Teeth College, she'd lose her trust fund."

The dark fairy clenched her fist and banged it on the table, making the crystal ball vibrate and nearly tumble off. "It's that kind of disdain for us as tooth fairies and the bad reputation we have that my students are rebelling against."

"It's your school and way of doing things that have earned you that reputation," Willow argued, not backing down.

"I can't believe that Courtney has money, and this is the first I've heard of it," Headmistress Sham seethed, mostly to herself.

"She *had* money," Paris corrected. "She's been cut off."

Willow nodded. "I think there are at least two more students involved, based on what I've heard. Courtney, Sidney, and Whitney are often seen together on Roya Lane. Aren't they here too?"

"Whitney isn't involved," Headmistress Sham said with conviction.

"I'm not sure you can confirm that without a doubt," Willow argued.

"You've given me zero proof of any of this," the tooth fairy stated. "I can't go around accusing students without evidence."

"Courtney's wand broke," Paris stated. "I'm telling you that I was there when it happened. How would I know that otherwise?"

"Well, but still, Whitney is innocent until proven otherwise." Headmistress Sham lifted her chin and looked directly at Willow. "If you truly want to resolve the root of this issue, then you and I must fix the underlying tensions between our colleges. Then Queen Helena MacGillie will be pleased, and we will all be happy."

Willow pushed back from the table, letting out a long breath. "No, not all of us will be happy. I refuse to condone what you do. You understand that my condition to accept and associate with you hasn't changed."

Headmistress Sham launched to her feet, staring daggers down at the fairy godmother. "Oh, you're simply impossible and so uptight I want to murder you."

CHAPTER THIRTY-SEVEN

Reflexively Paris bolted to a standing position, moving into a protective position between Headmistress Sham and Willow. The crow cawed, but the tooth fairy didn't budge. To Paris' surprise, neither did Willow seem unnerved by the threat.

"You know that murdering me would only make your plight worse," the fairy godmother said calmly at Paris' back, the words intended for the tooth fairy. "Without me, you'd be forced out of the bubble. It's only because of my support that Saint Valentine hasn't pushed to have you kicked out of here."

"He has no power," Headmistress Sham argued, but there was real fear in her eyes.

"You know that he does," Willow said. "And once kicked out, where will the tooth fairies go?"

"We would find a place," Headmistress Sham stated, but there was no confidence in her voice.

"We all know that I have the support of my leader, Saint Valentine, when it comes to locations and money," Willow replied in a conceited tone Paris had never heard her use. "Where is your leader?"

"M-M-Merlin has had other things to attend to," the tooth fairy stuttered, suddenly flustered.

"Merlin has stayed strung out on dark magic for centuries, and we both know it," Willow countered. "That's why you're alone. I bet you do all the assignments as well as the education of all the tooth fairies. He offers you no resources, which is why you need the subsidies from Queen Helena MacGillie.

"Your leader has left you, and we both know it. He can't help you defend your position in the bubble, protected from the world and with a location. He can't give you resources. The one who was supposed to help you accomplish your job filling the wellspring with magical power has abandoned you."

Paris had never seen this type of confidence in Headmistress Starr. Plus, this was all brand-new information to her. So she decided to stand aside and hear what else she didn't know about these two groups of fairies.

Then the most unexpected thing happened. The big dark fairy broke down, tumbling back into the rickety chair and crying, her head falling into her hands. "You don't understand. We've been cut off. This place is falling apart. We have no money and people see us as rejects. We're alone."

Paris felt sorry for Headmistress Sham and the tooth fairies, but apparently, Willow didn't.

The fairy godmother shook her head. "You chose how to fill the Fang Wellspring. I warned you that I wouldn't condone it."

"We're tooth fairies!" Headmistress Sham exclaimed, tears falling down her face. "What are we supposed to do? That's what Merlin assigned us for. I can't change it now even if he doesn't return my calls. I can only do so much with so little."

"Don't you see what the dark magic is doing?" Willow argued. "You're dark. You're hurting yourself. It's slow, but it's happening."

"You could never put up with a little of it," the tooth fairy said in a mocking voice.

"How could I?" Willow challenged.

"What we create fulfills our purposes," Headmistress Sham stated. "We created magical power."

"You can create all sorts of power, but that doesn't mean it's pure or good," Willow stated. "That's why I won't mend things with you. That's why we can't get along. And that's why you won't get the funding you want from the Seelie queen."

The dark fairy sighed. "Well, again we're at an impasse because I don't know how to fix what you want."

"I realize that," Willow said. "That's not why I'm here. I simply want you to intervene and discipline your fairies. Make them stop harassing my grounds. If you do, I won't ask Saint Valentine to take further action."

"You still have no further evidence of who is behind this," Headmistress Sham argued. "I can't simply accuse my students, or they'll drop out left and right. I'm already losing enrollment. I've lost some recently, and that was after taking in those who weren't pure fairies."

"I've taken in some non-fairies too," Willow stated.

Headmistress Sham glanced at Paris. "Yes, I see that."

"And others," Willow countered.

"Well, then you're more open-minded than you used to be." Headmistress Sham looked impressed.

"If we get you evidence, you'll intervene, is that right?" Willow asked.

The other fairy nodded.

"Until then, will you open the lines of communications with me so we can work toward peace?" Willow questioned. "We might not be able to mend things under the current circumstances, but we can at least try to get along, right?"

The dark fairy nodded. "It's really all I've wanted for so long. But I don't know how to operate the way you would approve of. Our job is to create magic, and the way to do that was taking teeth and converting them to power in the wellspring."

"Which creates dark magic," Willow stated.

"Therefore, again, we're at an impasse."

"Still, let's try and resolve the fighting." Willow handed the other fairy a card. "That's my direct line. Call me with any information, and I'll do the same."

CHAPTER THIRTY-EIGHT

P aris and Willow didn't meet any other tooth fairies on their way out of the grounds of Loose Teeth College. Most of the students did mind Headmistress Sham—not the Knees, though. It was up to Headmistress Starr to prove that those students were attacking Happily Ever After College to get Headmistress Sham to take action. Paris hoped that either the Knees cooled it or that it was easy to get evidence of their antics. She wasn't holding out hope on the first part.

"How did it go?" Sophia asked when Willow and Paris came through the vortex door, back into the juniper forest.

"We met some trouble." Paris brushed off her leather jacket, noticing that one of the fireballs had burned it.

Willow smiled at her proudly. "Thankfully, because of Paris, we were safe."

"I used fireball magic for the first time," Paris admitted to her aunt, trying to hide her pride.

"Cool." Lunis rose from where he was lying, gnawing on a dead tree trunk like a dog toy. "I'll take one."

Paris blinked at him in surprise, wondering if this was some dragon thing she didn't know about. "You want me to give you a fireball. What for?"

"I'm thirsty," he answered, his tongue hanging out his mouth, again reminding her of a dog.

Sophia rolled her eyes at her dragon. "She means fireball as in the hot round thing. Not the cinnamon whiskey."

He shook his head, looking disappointed. "Oh, well never mind. That won't taste good at all. I have my fire, thanks very much."

"Did you apprehend the culprits?" Sophia asked.

Paris shook her head. "Like the cowards they are, they fled when I nearly lit them on fire and knocked them off a mausoleum with some wind."

"Wow, it sounds like y'all had all the fun," Lunis said with a defeated sigh. "All we did was sit here and count the branches on that tree." He nodded in the direction of the trunk he'd been gnawing on moments prior.

"Some of us did that," Sophia countered. "Some of us took the time to catch up on email and record the electromagnetic vibrations coming from the vortex fields here."

"Some of us are nerds," Lunis said in a suddenly nasal voice, sniffing and taking his large, clawed hand and pretending to push glasses up on his snout.

"Some of us are ridiculous, and when they got bored of wasting their time, they tore up the tree whose branches they'd been counting." Sophia laughed and leaned in Paris' direction. "I don't think he can count that high."

"There is no number after ninety-tree," Lunis argued, making everyone laugh.

"So were you able to meet with Headmistress Sham at Loose Teeth College?" Sophia asked after they'd settled down.

Willow smiled pleasantly. "We did, and although I think we made progress, bringing the situation with the rebellious students to her attention, she won't intervene until we can prove they're behind the attacks."

"Speaking of teeth," Lunis cut in. "You know what's gray and bad for your teeth?"

Sophia groaned and glanced at Paris and Willow. "It's less painful if you play along." She glanced up at her dragon. "What is gray and bad for your teeth?"

"A boulder," Lunis answered and roared with laughter at his joke.

"Can you get Headmistress Sham to at least monitor her student's behavior more closely?" Sophia asked, returning her attention to the fairy godmother.

"As I feared," Willow began, "there is still much tension between us. Headmistress Sham is still very bitter about being cut off from the Seelie Court and won't do me any favors until the queen reinstates her funding."

"Well, then it sounds like a simple matter of arbitration, which is the Dragon Elite's specialty," Sophia stated proudly. "Usually, it's a matter of one side needing one thing to agree to peace. So what is it you need to mend relations with Loose Teeth College?"

"Speaking of the tooth fairies," Lunis interrupted with a serious look. "Do you know why you should never brush your teeth with your left hand?"

"We're trying to do something here," Sophia spat at the blue dragon.

"I'm trying to offer helpful advice," he said smugly.

"Okay, fine," Sophia acquiesced. "Why should you never brush your teeth with your left hand?"

He rolled his eyes. "Duh, because a toothbrush works better."

This time no one laughed.

Sophia lowered her chin and regarded Lunis with hooded eyes. "Is that the last one?"

"It's hard to say." He glanced at Willow. "Why are you at odds with the tooth fairies?"

"Because what they create is dark magic," Willow answered. "Converting children's teeth to magic produces a flawed source in the Fang Wellspring."

"But that's their job, right?" Sophia asked. "Because fairies don't have a readily available source of magic like magicians."

Willow nodded. "As well as some other species like giants and gnomes. Although they offer them a source, it often creates more problems than it solves because the magic is so volatile."

"Is the problem in that they steal the teeth from children?" Sophia asked. "Is that what makes the magic dark?"

"Speaking of children," Lunis cut in once more. "What do you call a bear with no teeth?"

"I don't see what bears have to do with children," Sophia argued.

"Just go along with it," he encouraged.

"Fine," Sophia stated. "What do you call a bear with no teeth?"

"A gummy bear!" Lunis exclaimed, rolling over and laughing.

"Anyway." Sophia looked at the headmistress. "Back to the business at hand."

Willow shook her head. "I don't think the problem is that the tooth fairies take the teeth from children. They don't need them anymore so at least they aren't taking them from someone who would."

Paris shivered at the notion of stealing teeth from adult's mouths. "The problem is that the flaws in the teeth, which are inevitable, create flaws in the magic, then?"

Willow affirmed this with a nod. "Yes, converting teeth into magic to fuel the wellspring is a good idea in theory, but it's too unstable a material. Because they take them from children who are often mischievous, the teeth produce volatile magic. Once in the Fang Wellspring, it all mixes and creates a darker source of power."

"So even if there's magic from a good kid who goes to the dentist," Paris said slowly, working it out in her head as she spoke, "then one bad tooth spoils the whole lot."

"Speaking of the dentist," Lunis interrupted. "My dentist mocked me the other day, saying that although he's much older than me, he has healthier teeth."

Sophia sucked in a patient breath. "Then what did you say?"

"I told him it must be because he has a better dentist." Lunis rolled around some more in the dirt, laughing.

"I apologize," Sophia said to Paris and Willow. "Lun appears to be on a roll."

"On a roll," the blue dragon repeated as he laughed and continued to roll around on the ground.

"So, what if there was a quality assurance process for the teeth they converted to magic?" Sophia asked Willow.

"I asked Headmistress Sham to consider that at one point," Willow began. "She said that she didn't have the resources for such things. I'll even admit that the process would be intensive and probably not work entirely. Then as Paris said, one bad tooth pollutes the entire wellspring, producing dark and unpredictable magic."

"So the solution is to clean the wellspring," Lunis offered, having gone back to gnawing on the tree trunk. Not looking up, he continued as if he was talking to himself.

"The problem isn't in taking the teeth. If they're a source that creates magic, there's no use in reinventing the wheel to find another element. Therefore you need to run a net through the Fang Wellspring like one does a pool before taking a swim. Then you get out all the dirt or whatnot, and you can dive in."

All three of the women blinked at Lunis in surprise.

"That's a brilliant solution," Willow said after a long pause, her mouth hanging open and eyes wide.

"It's why I keep him around." Sophia smiled at her dragon. "Despite his bad jokes, he can surprise me with fantastic advice."

"Oh, and also because I could eat you." Lunis continued to chew on the wood.

"The problem is," Willow said, a puzzled look on her face. "I don't have enough capability to clean something like the Fang Wellspring. I'm certain that Headmistress Sham doesn't either. It's beyond our scope."

"Unfortunately, I don't think the Dragon Elite or the House of Fourteen can help you there either," Sophia said regretfully. "Fairy magic is very different from ours as magicians, and I fear that we'd only make the problem worse."

"I know exactly who could clean the Fang Wellspring." A broad grin appeared on Paris' face as the idea she'd been working out finally unwove fully in her mind—all the pieces fitting together.

"Who?" Willow, Sophia, and Lunis asked in unison.

Paris pointed at the fourth quadrant on the medicine wheel that led the vortex door she hadn't been through yet. "The Seelie queen."

CHAPTER THIRTY-NINE

"That's impossible," Willow said at once in protest to Paris' idea. "There's no way she'd do it."

"Usually, most things people think are impossible are only improbable." Lunis stood and swished his long tail.

Sophia nodded at her dragon. "Yes, everyone has a price. What's the queen's?"

"That's not the beginning of the issue," Willow argued. "I can't be granted permission to speak to Queen Helena MacGillie. She's forbidden either the fairy godmothers or the tooth fairies to enter her court."

Sophia chewed on her lip. "Well, I don't think that Lunis and I can help you there. As non-fairies, we are especially not allowed in the fairy court."

"How would Queen Helena MacGillie know if you and Head-mistress Sham mended relations?" Paris asked Willow.

"She would," the fairy godmother answered. "The Seelie can sense harmony."

"Of course she would..." Paris muttered.

"It's true that Queen Helena MacGillie does have the power to clean the Fang Wellspring, right?" Sophia asked.

"Yes, I believe so," Willow answered.

"Then it would be a clean source of magic," Lunis stated.

"Then you would mend fences with the tooth fairies, and the queen of the Seelie would be happy," Paris offered. "Loose Teeth College gets its funding. The fairy godmothers can rest assured because the wellspring has clean magic and the Seelie have peace between their neighbors. It's a win, win, win."

"That's a lot of wins." Lunis laughed.

"Where's the joke, Lun?" Sophia questioned, putting her hands on her hip and pursing her lips at her dragon.

He huffed. "Sometimes there isn't one. I can be serious."

"No, you can't," Sophia argued, eyeing the dragon who wore an ultra-serious expression.

"It's not going to work," he said through clenched teeth as if refraining himself. "I'm not going to break and tell a joke on winning."

"Fine." Sophia returned her attention to Willow. "So it sounds like you have to take the risk and enter the Seelie Court to ask Queen Helena MacGillie to clean the wellspring. Then Headmistress Sham will be more amenable and stop her students from attacking Happily Ever After College."

"You don't understand," Willow said with urgency. "If I set foot in that land, I'll be captured and killed. The queen made it clear that she's banned both the fairy godmothers and the tooth fairies from her court. As much as the Seelie value harmony, they can be very malicious and dangerous."

Paris pulled out the letter Father Time gave her. "I think I have an exception."

CHAPTER FORTY

"What's that?" Willow ran her gaze over the envelope.

"It's from Papa Creola." Sophia recognized the wax seal with the father of time's insignia.

Paris nodded, holding up the envelope and turning it over. "He gave this to me and told me to give it to Queen Helena MacGillie. It's addressed to her."

"Let's read it." Lunis' head on his long neck suddenly draped low next to the letter.

Paris snatched it away from his prying eyes and wide mouth of sharp teeth. "No."

"Wait, Papa Creola asked you to give Queen Helena MacGillie a letter from him?" Willow asked. "Why?"

"He didn't say," Paris stated. "But I'm guessing it says something like, 'Don't kill Willow and Paris.'"

"Open it, and let's see," Lunis said eagerly.

Again, Paris held the envelope back away from the dragon. "No. I've been thinking about visiting the Seelie Court since learning of the tensions and problems between the fairies. She must be a part of the solution. Papa Creola wants the solution too because he helped me speed up part of my school project so I could deliver this letter."

Willow scratched her head, overwhelmed by this new development. "So you think that letter will keep us from getting killed?"

"I think it will buy us some time," Paris answered. "It will be up to our smooth and quick talking to keep from getting killed. We have to present this solution quickly and in a way that appeals to the queen."

"She'll be furious at us for trespassing," Willow countered. "The Seelie and Unseelie are very difficult fairies. They're constantly playing tricks and looking for ways to deceive. So even if we survive long enough to get an audience with the queen, that doesn't mean we're out of danger."

"Yeah, the Seelie and Unseelie will see you as fresh meat," Lunis teased.

"The alternative is that the feud continues," Paris argued, giving Willow a pleading expression. "Don't you want the Fang Wellspring cleaned up?"

"Of course I do," she answered at once.

"Then we have to take the risk," Paris stated with determination, holding up the letter. "Papa Creola has given us a way into the court. We have to deliver this letter."

"It's probably a bill," Lunis joked. "The Seelie queen is going to murder you on the spot when she opens it."

Sophia rolled her eyes. "I'm sure you won't be the bearer of bad news. The letter is probably like you said, Pare, and it permits you to enter or pleads your case."

"Or it's a ransom note," Lunis offered. "All cut-up pieces of letters from a magazine saying that King Rudolf Sweetwater will be given back to the Seelie unless they meet Papa Creola's demands."

Paris laughed. "That's a possibility. Papa Creola would want to get rid of Rudolf."

Willow chewed on her lip, her gaze distant in thought. "You do have a letter addressed to Queen Helena MacGillie from Papa Creola. It would be wrong not to ensure that she gets it."

"The only way to get it to her is to enter her court," Paris added, her tone laced with persuasion.

"That's true." Willow still wavered with indecision.

"If you don't come back, can I have your squirrel?" Lunis asked Paris.

Sophia slapped him playfully on the side. "She's coming back."

"But if she doesn't," he argued. "You know how much I want a talking squirrel."

"You want everything," Sophia argued, offering Paris an encouraging smile. "You go through and message me if you have trouble. I'll send King Rudolf after you or do whatever I can to help, although that man might make things worse...it's always hard to tell."

Paris nodded, turning to Willow. "What do you say? Ready for another adventure? I'll be the muscle if you'll be the sweet-talker?"

To her surprise, Willow smiled and nodded with confidence. "Yes, and I think we make a good team. Let's do it."

Following the fairy godmother, Paris made her way over to the fourth quadrant on the medicine wheel.

"Hey, Pare," Lunis said before she stepped into the vortex door that led to the Seelie and Unseelie Court. "Yo mama's teeth are so yellow..."

"How yellow are they?" She'd learned to encourage the blue dragon's jokes.

"Liv's teeth are so yellow that she stood on the street corner and smiled, and traffic slowed down."

Paris laughed, stepping into the quadrant that led to the Seelie and Unseelie Courts, hoping this was a good idea and she wasn't leading Willow and herself to their death.

CHAPTER FORTY-ONE

As soon as the vortex door dropped Paris into the land of the Seelie and Unseelie, she knew she was in a strange and amazing place...that was also very dangerous.

The first thing Paris felt was the snow falling from the purple sky. That would've been bizarre on its own, but it was falling on beautiful green grass, spring flowers, and fertile land of lush trees where it melted immediately. The temperature was warm as if it was a hot summer day, although the snow made it feel like winter.

Reading the confusion on Paris' face, Willow offered an understanding smile. "They have all the seasons in the land of the Seelie and Unseelie."

"I guess that makes sense," Paris reasoned, remembering that the different seasons represented the two different types of fairies.

Besides the fact that snow was falling while the sun was scorching, the land around them didn't seem so strange. Well, if one was used to the Bewilder Forest, maybe. A patch of daisies had faces in their middles and was holding an earnest conversation by the sounds of it. Next to the flowers, two rabbits appeared to be playing a game of cards. In the tree overhead was a raccoon smoking a cigar.

Paris rubbed her eyes, wondering when someone slipped her the hallucinogens.

Willow leaned over and whispered, "Don't talk to the owls. They lie about everything."

"Riiiiight." Paris watched as an owl swooped down from a branch and took the spot on the ground before them.

"Are you looking for something?" The large brown bird's beak moved with its words, making it appear more like a puppet than an actual talking animal. Since Paris' best friend was a squirrel who could wax on about science, this shouldn't have been weird for her, but it still was.

"That's okay." Willow brushed past the owl and waved at Paris to follow.

"If you follow the river, you're bound to find whatever you're looking for." The owl hopped to keep up with them.

"If the owls lie, does that mean we don't follow the river?" Paris murmured to Willow.

The fairy godmother looked undecided. "It's hard to say, but I think we should stay away from the river." She pointed at a stream in the distance. It carried purple liquid that matched the strange sky.

"Lie!" the owl hooted. "We don't lie! Well, Siri does. And Dipidous. But not me!"

"Siri and Dipidous?" Paris questioned. "When they're together, is it serendipitous?"

The owl batted his eyelashes at her, appearing offended. "No, it is nothing of the sort."

"What's your name?" Paris was too curious not to ask despite Willow's warning not to converse with the owls. She didn't see what the harm was if she didn't believe them.

"Cleveland." The owl looked to the side. "Anyway, where are you headed?"

"Go away, Cleveland." Willow shooed the owl away with her hand as she paused to look around. The land was as diverse as the weather with rolling green hills around them, snow-capped mountains in the distance, a stream that jutted back and forth and disappeared over a cliff to the west, and a dense forest to the east. Where they'd come through at the vortex door, there was a desert sprinkled with cacti of various sizes and shapes.

"I think the Seelie Court is that way on the other side of those trees." Willow pointed toward the forest.

"Oh, you're going to the Seelie Court, then?" Cleveland asked. "The queen will be so happy to see you."

"No, she won't, and we both know it," Willow spat, taking off for the forest, which Paris thought would hold lots more strangeness and possible dangers.

"Well, that's not the way to the Seelie Court." Cleveland launched into the air, flew several yards, and turned to look at them. He nodded at the desert. "Everyone knows that the Seelie Court is twenty paces that way."

"I can plainly see that it's not." Willow hurried along.

"Oh, that's only because a mirage hides it," Cleveland explained.

Willow paused, considering this. Then she shook her head. "No, you're trying to fool us. I know how you owls work."

"We work to help you," he argued. "You're untrusting, which says more about you and your issues than about us."

Another owl swooped down from the trees as they entered the path of the forest and landed next to Cleveland. "Hey, Gerald. Who are your friends?"

Willow halted, glaring at the owls. "Cleveland, huh?" She turned to Paris. "I told you that the owls lie. We're better off ignoring them. They want to confuse us."

"Help you," Cleveland, or rather Gerald, corrected and turned his head to face the other one. "Go away, Siri. Don't you have jury duty?"

"The queen let me off for the day," Siri answered.

"What's the fate of the fairy on trial?" he asked.

"Guilty!" Siri stated. "Off with their head."

"What?" Paris asked, her and Willow not having moved off yet, too curious about what the owls were talking about. "What did this fairy do?"

"Oh, she wore green on a Tuesday," Siri replied.

Paris gave Willow a skeptical look. "I'm guessing that's a lie."

Willow shook her head. "No, that's probably close to the truth. It might be that she wore red on a Wednesday, but that sounds like something Queen Helena MacGillie would do."

"I thought the Seelie were good compared to the Unseelie," Paris argued.

"They are," Willow began. "The Unseelie don't have trials. Their king accuses and kills criminals on the spot."

Paris gulped, wondering if this was a good idea after all. She glanced down. "Is it illegal to wear black on Thursday?"

Siri replied "Yes" at the exact same time that Gerald said, "No."

"Which is it?" Paris asked, giving Willow a troubled look.

The fairy godmother shook her head. "Don't worry. If we're getting beheaded, it's for showing up. Our clothes won't be the offense."

"You're not a member of the court," Siri explained, butting into their conversation. "So no one cares what you wear."

Gerald snickered at this, hiding his expression by turning his head halfway around.

Paris rolled her eyes. "So that means it does matter what we wear."

Willow nodded. "In the Seelie Court, it always matters what you wear. Let's hope the letter from Papa Creola is good enough to keep us out of trouble."

"Oh, a letter from the father of time." Siri batted her eyelashes and suddenly looked interested. "I can deliver it for you."

Paris shook her head. "No, Hedwig. We're good. Fly along. We're fine without your help."

The owl stuck its beak in the air, now offended. "Fine. Now I'm going to warn the queen that you're here. I bet you don't have a chance to show her the letter before she strikes you dead."

Before Paris could protest, the owl launched into the air and flew farther into the forest.

She gave Willow a foreboding expression. "That can't be good…"

Willow nodded, sharing her anxiety. "At least we know we're

headed in the right direction. Let's hurry before the queen has a chance to load the cannons."

"Please tell me that's an expression, and Queen Helena MacGillie doesn't really have cannons…"

Willow gave her an apologetic look over her shoulder as she hurried down the path through the forest. "I'm afraid not."

CHAPTER FORTY-TWO

To Paris' surprise, there weren't too many interruptions in the forest as they progressed deeper. The raccoons blew smoke down on them, making Paris cough and wave her hand to fan the thick aroma off her. However, other than overhearing the strange conversations from the daisies who seemed to be discussing a proposed new tax bill and other topics on politics, there wasn't much else of interest.

"The laws in the forest are stricter," Willow explained when she caught Paris looking around for lurking danger. "We're probably safest in here. Most don't venture through here because they don't want to get caught tripping on their feet or misusing a word."

"Grammar errors are illegal?" Paris asked. "No wonder there are so many solitaries who have split from the Seelie and the Unseelie."

Willow nodded. "The laws here are very arbitrary, but those who remain like the benefits that come with living here so they chance it."

"Which are?" Paris asked.

"Well, for one, all indulgences are allowed and encouraged," Willow stated. "The Seelie and Unseelie, much like the fae, indulge their every desire. They also enjoy the whimsical nature of the land."

"It's quite the interesting place," Paris remarked as they passed a pair of chipmunks that were playing darts on a tree stump, throwing them at a target in the distance.

"There's no place like it," Willow agreed. "For most, the Seelie and Unseelie here are bonded to their home. Outside of their land, if they were on Roya Lane, for instance, they would be policed by the Fairy Law Enforcement Agency for deceiving others or making people fall into agreements without their knowledge. Here they're allowed to do as they wish without consequence for all their deception."

"Yeah, but you can't wear green on a Tuesday," Paris argued.

"Yes, but they like the strange laws because that's part of indulging their whimsical nature," Willow explained. "The Seelie and Unseelie thrive on uncertainty and enjoy that their rulers change the laws on a moment's notice and without warning."

"These fairies are wack," Paris stated.

Willow nodded. "Yes, it's probably because they're Scottish."

"Well, that explains it."

"Oh, there's the entrance to the court." Willow pointed at a gate that was visible through the trees up ahead.

The pair hurried, hoping to beat the queen before she loaded up too many weapons for their arrival.

CHAPTER FORTY-THREE

A s they neared, Paris noticed that the golden gates with their intricate design connected to a tall hedge on either side. Gold bricks formed the path that started on the other side of the gates. Paris had known since coming through the vortex door that they weren't in Kansas anymore, but she didn't think they were in Oz now based on the yellow brick road. She was reasonably sure the bricks were real gold and the gates too. These fairies were very indulgent and had expensive tastes.

"Follow my lead," Willow whispered as they approached the gates.

When Paris and Willow entered the court, a hush fell over the area, which was filled with people and animals. The court was a square with beautiful fairies lining the green hedge walls. They were all dressed as if they were going to a ball with large gowns covered in sparkles and feathers or lavish suits in velvet and silk.

The court was open although columns connected by marble archways lined the back wall. Siri was hopping around next to a woman who stood at the front of the court and wore a murderous expression. She was incredibly beautiful with long blonde hair. Her long white gown had silver feathers around the hips and a corset made of platinum.

Sprouting from her shoulders were two silver wings that flitted and in her hand was a tall scepter. As Paris expected, a large crown covered in stunning diamonds sat on Queen Helena's head. Unexpectedly, two huge blue butterflies held up the train of her long white gown behind her, as if she was about to walk down the aisle at her wedding.

Around the queen of the Seelie were her noble court and beside them at their feet were various animals, such as foxes wearing button-up vests and ferrets with top hats. Most of the animals were small, save for one large stag with massive antlers, which was chewing and blowing pink bubble gum.

Paris wondered if she'd accidentally ingested a drug when she entered the land of the Seelie and Unseelie. However, she shook off the strangeness all around her as she followed Willow's lead. They progressed straight into the court with confidence, not deterred by the silence or the penetrating eyes staring at them from all angles. Or the fact that the queen had narrowed her eyes and appeared moments away from pointing her staff at them, killing them on the spot.

When they were only a few yards from Queen Helena MacGillie, Willow dropped into a low bow on one knee. Paris, holding the letter from Papa Creola, copied the movement.

Paris wondered why the headmistress wasn't saying something. Why she hadn't charged into the court, announcing that they had a letter for the queen from Father Time.

The silence was deafening and went on for too long. Paris slid her eyes to the side, noticing that Willow continued to hang her head low and keep her lips tightly closed.

"Sooooo," Queen Helena MacGillie said. "You may stand now and speak, but I warn you that your death is inevitable. I've only allowed you to live this long because I'm bored and want to know why you're suddenly suicidal when that's never been your way, Willow Starr."

Her accent was a thick Scottish one which made her words sound polite although she was severely angry.

In her peripheral vision, Paris noticed as the fairy godmother rose. She copied the movement. She guessed that one of the many laws must be that one had to bow and not speak first when meeting the Seelie queen. Willow probably saved them from being killed right away. If it were Paris, she would've charged in there yelling, "I have a letter for you from Papa Creola." Queen Helena MacGillie probably would've shot her down before she finished the sentence.

The Seelie queen smiled wickedly, her eyes running over the headmistress and Paris. "Oh, and you brought me a pet. I've always wanted a halfling. She will look so nice in that cage."

She pointed her scepter at one corner. Paris noticed a large gold cage that currently imprisoned a monkey. Gulping, she hoped that this worked. Otherwise, she'd gotten Willow murdered and would be the queen's pet for the rest of her life.

CHAPTER FORTY-FOUR

"Queen Helena MacGillie, I know that I'm not allowed to enter your lands," Willow began, her chin held high and her voice steady. "But I have a good reason for my visit and would like the opportunity to present it to you."

Again, Paris would have simply thrust the letter with the queen's name on it in the air, waving the envelope and saying, "Papa Creola sent this for you!"

However, there appeared to be formalities when it came to the Seelie queen, and Willow had told Paris to follow her lead. Therefore she kept her mouth shut and the letter pressed between her fingers by her side.

Queen Helena MacGillie considered the request. "I will listen to your reason but only if you make your halfling stick out her tongue. I only want her if she's healthy."

"She isn't my halfling, and you can make the requests directly to her." Willow looked at Paris.

At this, there was the first bit of muttering from the crowd around them.

"So she isn't your servant?" Queen Helena MacGillie asked. "I thought that halflings were usually born without a brain due to their flawed genetics."

"My genetics aren't flawed!" Paris exclaimed, unable to control the outburst.

The court of fairies gasped, most of them drawing back in sudden shock.

Willow flinched as if she expected the queen to shoot her down on the spot.

Instead, the queen brandished an amused smile. "I like my pets to have a little attitude. I won't cut off one of your hands for the outburst since I'm surprised you can talk."

Willow cleared her throat, attempting a polite smile. "Paris is the first of her kind. Therefore, anything you've heard about halflings doesn't apply to her. I assure you she's a very intelligent woman."

"Tongue, halfling!" the Seelie queen ordered. "I want to see it!"

Paris restrained the urge to roll her eyes and dutifully slid her tongue out of her mouth, showing it to Queen Helena MacGillie.

"Oh, yes, very healthy indeed," the queen said, impressed. "Although you should eat more fruits and fewer carbohydrates. Also, you'll need two to three steam baths a day to clear your pores."

Paris pulled her tongue back into her mouth and shut it before she said anything else she'd regret that would get them killed.

Turning her focus back on Willow, Queen Helena feigned a pleased smile. "Okay, go on then. Tell me why you've broken my laws, entering my land. Your answer will dictate how you die, but I assure you that regardless of the reason, today will be your last, Willow Starr. I can't let such an offense go, or I'll lose complete respect with my people."

CHAPTER FORTY-FIVE

Paris wanted to protest right away, but Willow cut her off.

"I understand," the headmistress stated at once, nodding like her death as a punishment was completely reasonable. "I thought that would be the case and accept my fate. There was no other way to ensure that you got a very important letter."

She held out her hand, not glancing at Paris, but the intention obvious. Dutifully Paris laid the letter from Papa Creola in the fairy godmother's palm.

Not taking her eyes off the Seelie queen, Willow held the letter into the air, the seal with the insignia visible. "I have a letter from Papa Creola that he asked Paris to deliver to you personally." She turned the envelope over, showing the other side where the father of time had written the queen's name.

Queen Helena MacGillie's eyes widened with shock. Many around the court began whispering. One of the butterflies holding up her train flew closer as if it was hoping to read the letter over her shoulder.

"Well, then have your halfling deliver it," Queen Helena MacGillie ordered.

Willow glanced at Paris, handed her back the letter, and gave her an encouraging nod.

Paris thought that her feet might slide out from under her when she attempted to take the next step, her nervousness making her knees wobbly. That was probably against the law and would get her beheaded before she could hand over the missive.

"Here you are, Queen Helena MacGillie." Paris bowed as she handed the letter to the Seelie.

She yanked the letter from Paris' hands greedily, her eyes narrowed on her. Her gaze ran over her name on the front of the envelope as if she was trying to decide if the writing matched Papa Creola's. Further scrutiny was paid to the wax seal when she flipped the letter over.

Paris held her breath, not taking her spot next to Willow but rather hoping to spy what the letter said, much like the curious butterfly.

Not paying her anymore notice, the queen slid a fingernail through the seal, breaking it easily. Gracefully she pulled the flap open and yanked a piece of thick parchment out. Paris couldn't make out a single word from the other side of the paper, but she could tell there weren't many on the page. It appeared to be a single sentence.

Queen Helena MacGillie slid her eyes over the words, and her eyes darted to Paris—complete awe written in her gaze.

"You," she said in the sudden hush. "You're the one we've been waiting for."

CHAPTER FORTY-SIX

"Say what?" Paris asked over the sudden loud ruckus of gasps and exclamations all around the court.

"It's her!" someone yelled.

The fox ran over and sniffed at her shoes, looking up at her with large brown eyes.

The stag popped a bubble, making many jump.

Paris glanced back at Willow, but the headmistress' confused expression told her that she didn't know what this was all about.

"You've been waiting on me for what?" Paris looked back at the queen, hoping that they hadn't been waiting on her to feast on her body or be their forever prisoner or dance monkey.

"According to Papa Creola, you are the one who will finally settle the dispute." Queen Helena MacGillie turned the piece of parchment around to reveal the words on it.

They read: *The halfling is the key to creating peace between the Seelie and the Unseelie.*

Tension knit in Paris' chest. She had no idea how that could be the case. She had just entered this land.

"Of course." Willow took the place next to Paris, sudden understanding on her face. "Paris as a halfling with demon blood is perfect for the job."

"Why would that matter?" Paris asked.

"Because the Seelie and Unseelie are opposite," Willow explained. "One is light and the other dark. You are opposites as a half-magician and half-fairy. You have both the cognitive predisposition of a magician and the emotional tendency of a fairy. Also, your demon blood makes you edgy, much like the Unseelie, which have never been accepted by most in the magical world, always seen as rebels."

"That is good reasoning, Willow." Queen Helena MacGillie nodded.

This was all overwhelming to Paris. First, she found out that she was the key to the fairy godmother's survival. Now she was learning that she was vital to creating peace between the Seelie and Unseelie fairies. Talk about pressure. Still, it made sense based on what Willow was saying.

"Well, I'm not going to do anything to help you if you harm Willow," Paris said boldly. "I'll only create peace between you and the Unseelie if you promise not to harm her."

The Seelie queen wasn't used to being told what she could and couldn't do based on the look of horror on her face. The second round of gasps from the court echoed around Paris.

Queen Helena MacGillie opened her mouth but didn't say a word.

Paris seized her opportunity, taking the power she thought owed her based on this turn of events. "Willow has a request to make of you that I think could benefit everyone. Only if you do it will I help you and the Unseelie."

The queen's face flushed a violent shade of red. All eyes were on her. Not a single breath seemed to leave anyone's lungs as they watched and waited for Queen Helena MacGillie's response.

"Do you have any other demands?" she finally asked, her eyes narrowed into small slits.

Paris thought about it, wondering if she could up the ante, but decided that their survival and cleaning the Fang Wellspring was enough. She was about to say that was it when Willow stepped forward.

"You can't kill Paris after she does what you've asked," she stated, giving her a sideways look.

That's right, Paris thought. The Seelie were very deceptive with their arrangements. Unless one explicitly stated things, there were all sorts of loopholes. Of course, the Seelie queen would want to murder the girl who'd made demands of her in front of her court after she'd gotten what she wanted.

After long deliberation, Queen Helena MacGillie nodded. "Very well, you two will remain safe. I'll grant your request, but besides having your help creating peace with the Unseelie, I will make one other demand of you."

"Which will be?" Paris asked.

"I'm not certain yet," the Seelie queen said. "First, I must know what it is you want me to do for you, Willow. That will dictate what I ask for. Do you agree?"

Willow glanced sideways at Paris again, and she gave a minute nod. "Okay," she answered, a sturdy expression on her face. "If you agree to help us, we'll help you."

The queen flashed a wicked smile. "Two centuries I've waited for the one who would bring peace between the Seelie and Unseelie. It is you, Paris Beaufont, who is key to restoring the balance between us according to the father of time, who I will not doubt on these matters. Tell me what you want me to do, and we can proceed finally after decades of constant warring."

CHAPTER FORTY-SEVEN

It was time for Paris to step back and allow Willow to speak. This was invariably about her and her college. However, Paris was willing to do whatever it took to help the Seelie, the Unseelie, the tooth fairies, and especially the fairy godmothers.

She never imagined that she'd be the key to all of the solutions. Still, even she had to admit that being a halfling provided her with a unique perspective and abilities. She was unlike anyone on Earth, and since learning this, she accepted that she'd have jobs unlike any other.

"I have come to you because I want to settle the long feud between Happily Ever After College and Loose Teeth College," Willow stated with confidence.

"But you haven't, or I would know," Queen Helena MacGillie said, authority in her tone.

Willow nodded. "I need your help to do it." She glanced at Paris beside her and bolstered her resolve. "We've come up with a solution that we think could mend relations between us."

"Why, after all this time, have you decided that you want to have peace?" the Seelie queen questioned, a skeptical glint in her eyes.

"Well, it's true that Headmistress Sham has wanted things resolved for quite some time."

"Of course," the queen chirped. "She wants my support."

Willow nodded. "Recently Happily Ever After College has been under attack by three tooth fairies. We believe that's how many, and we think we know who they are, although they've eluded us. Their resentments fuel them because fairy godmothers are wealthier than tooth fairies and have a better reputation. Headmistress Sham, although not approving of her students, will not help to enforce rules upon her students unless we mend relations."

The Seelie queen smiled wickedly, which made her both appear beautiful and dangerous. "She's a clever fairy. She has nothing much more to lose by doing nothing, but by forcing you to put the feud behind you to earn her protection, she gets what she wants."

An exasperated breath fell from the fairy godmother's lips. "I want to believe that this situation is forcing all of us to mend things and find peace amongst long bouts of turmoil."

"I think you're right," Queen Helena MacGillie stated. "It appears that by coming here with your halfling, that the Seelie and Unseelie might be close to a truce. As a bonus, the fairy godmothers and the tooth fairies might be as well. But it was you, Willow Starr, who moved Happily Ever After College and cut off ties from the tooth fairies—forcing me to ostracize both colleges. How is it that you've decided to put your grievances behind you?"

Willow drew in a breath, knitted her hands together, and lifted her chin. "I'm here to ask you to do us a favor to find a peaceful solution. It will be a gift, and you can't require anything paid back in return.

"We won't give you any of our firstborn children. You can't require centuries of servitude from our students. No other demand can be made. If you agree to do what I ask, you'll do it as a gift and promise to never ask for anything in return."

The Seelie queen had looked angry before when Paris had been so bold as to make her demands. Willow seemed to have stolen this page out of Paris' book. She couldn't be any prouder of the fairy godmother. However, she sorely hoped that this new confidence didn't get Willow killed.

Queen Helena MacGillie tightened her hand around her staff, her fingers going white. Her court all remained deathly silent as though afraid she might take her rage out on one of them if they dared to breathe too loudly all of a sudden.

Finally, she blinked her long eyelashes and forced a sinister smile that didn't quite reach her eyes. "What is it, this favor you request, Willow Starr?"

CHAPTER FORTY-EIGHT

"I want you to clean the Fang Wellspring so it doesn't have dark magic," Willow stated.

Muttering from the court broke out as the Seelie queen's expression remained neutral. Paris couldn't tell if Queen Helena MacGillie was offended or unimpressed by this request. However, a moment later, she got some clues from the owls who didn't keep their voices down.

"That will take a lot," Siri said to the one stationed beside him.

"It's a smart option," he replied. "Although a bold request."

"She'll never do it," Siri said, not in a whisper but talking over his shoulder like everyone couldn't hear him. Many in the court were whispering, but they seemed able to keep their volume down.

"She doesn't have a choice," the other owl stated. "If she wants the ugly halfling's help, the queen has to comply."

Having her patience run out, Paris shot the babbling owls a piercing look. "I can hear you, you ugly bag of feathers."

"At least we have wings," Siri hooted.

"I have wings," Paris argued, aware that everyone in the court was now looking at her and not the queen who still wore an unreadable expression.

"You glamour them like everyone outside our realm," Siri stated.

"They're useless and get in the way," Paris replied. She was about to say something else, but Willow laid a hand on her shoulder, pausing her.

"Don't let them goad you," she counseled. "That's what the owls like to do. They want you in contempt of the court so they have a job as a jury member."

"I'll give them a job," Paris threatened, narrowing her eyes at the owls. "You can be my dinner. I'd like you stuffed and served with a side of mashed potatoes."

Siri hooted uncomfortably, adjusting his wings suddenly as if he'd recently landed from a flight.

"Enough!" Queen Helena MacGillie boomed, making the court silent once more. "I have deliberated and decided that to strike an agreement, to achieve peace for all, with the fairy godmothers, I will clean the Fang Wellspring one time."

Willow pinched her mouth together, tension bouncing around in her eyes. "Actually, I need you to do it continuously. For eternity…"

CHAPTER FORTY-NINE

"I've always liked Willow Starr," a woman Seelie fairy said who wore a long red ball gown and had her brown hair pinned up high on her head like a beehive.

"Me too," a man as elegantly and fancifully dressed as her said at her side. "It's too bad she'll die."

"What will you wear to her funeral?" the woman asked, much like the owls, not bothering to keep her tone down as the Seelie queen fumed at the front of the court. Queen Helena's gaze was murderous.

If looks could kill, Paris thought, her fingers flexing by her side. She was ready to fight. To defend. To do whatever she needed to if the queen made the slightest move, although Paris was unsure if anything she could do would prove effective against the powerful Queen Helena MacGillie.

"It depends on if the service is in the morning or the afternoon," the man responded. "Maybe blue in honor of the fairy godmothers... well, unless that angers the queen. Then I'll wear the opposite of blue."

The woman nodded. "You look good in orange."

Paris glanced between Willow and the queen, wondering who was going to talk next. Or if Queen Helena MacGillie would tell the two loud idiots to shut up. It didn't appear as such. Willow seemed incapable of speaking all of a sudden, like the Seelie's icy gaze might have paralyzed her.

"Who do you think will replace Willow Starr?" the woman continued. "Surely not that ugly halfling who doesn't know how to dress."

"Would you two shut up," Paris threatened, breaking the spell locking the Seelie queen and Willow in a staring contest.

Queen Helena MacGillie darted her gaze over to the two babbling fairies. "If you ever wear orange to a funeral, I will ensure your heads are the centerpieces on the buffet table at the reception afterward."

They both nodded and took a sudden step back as if thinking that might take them out of the queen's striking zone.

"You're not going to kill Willow." Paris stepped toward the queen, protectively moving in front of the fairy godmother. "We made a deal. If you go back on it now, you can kiss your truce with the Unseelie goodbye. I won't ever help you if you harm the headmistress."

"Regularly cleaning the Fang Wellspring will require a lot of work on my part," the queen argued.

"Yes, but how much of your efforts are devoted to warring the Unseelie or protecting your people?" Paris countered, thinking that if they did battle often, that cost them a lot of energy and resources.

"It's true that the constant feuds are draining," the queen said.

All eyes darted back to Paris as though expecting her to volley back another argument. "So you clean the Fang Wellspring regularly since you're the only one powerful enough to ensure it doesn't have dark magic, and I'll settle the dispute with you and the Unseelie. You'll then be able to devote your energy to something that creates harmony rather than chaos. Isn't that more in line with your goals as the Seelie?"

The queen lowered her chin, drawing in a breath. "You are devilishly clever, halfling. I might understand why you're the key to our peace. You'll need that wit to deal with King Hamish Abernathy—the ruler of the Unseelie. Otherwise, I fear your soul will be split into a hundred pieces and sprinkled over his dinner."

Paris gulped, not looking forward to being this peace negotiator.

She guessed that she could do as foretold as she had with the Deathly Shadow, but that didn't mean it guaranteed her success.

When Paris didn't respond, the Seelie queen continued. "I have made my decision. You make a strong argument, and I would rather devote my power to creating a positive source of magic. Is it then agreed that if I keep the Fang Wellspring clean, then you, Willow Starr, will mend relations with Loose Teeth College—creating harmony once more?"

The fairy godmother stepped out from where Paris was shielding her and nodded. "Yes, I will keep things civil with Headmistress Sham once more."

"I do like this arrangement." The queen smiled. "It works for everyone, although there still is a problem that bothers me intensely."

"Which is?" Willow asked at once.

"These rebel tooth fairies," the queen answered. "They have broken into your land, attacked, and therefore must be punished."

"Well, Headmistress Sham offered to take care of them if I could provide evidence that they were the offenders," Willow explained. "If I end the feud, she will enforce her rule on her students, making it a punishable offense for attacking the fairy godmothers."

"That's not enough," the queen stated. "The fairy godmothers have minded their own business. I haven't liked that you've decided to split from the tooth fairies, but at least you kept to yourself. And Headmistress Sham, I know she'd like more than anything to end the skirmish.

"These students have stoked the fire. It's what brought us here, but not in the way I would've liked. It sounds as though they've created problems, and I can't condone lawbreakers. I must punish those who harm those who I value. Therefore, for me to clean the Fang Wellspring, you must apprehend these three students and bring them to me. Only then will I complete my end of the bargain. Then I will, in turn, expect the halfling to honor her side of the arrangement."

Queen Helena MacGillie turned her penetrating gaze on Paris. "Only then will yours and Willow's life be safe. Until then, know that I will watch you. I have ways of keeping my eyes on all who have been in my court. If I sense that you won't honor your side of our agreement to fix things between the Seelie and the Unseelie, I will cut my losses, quit cleaning the Fang Wellspring, and murder you and your headmistress instantly. Is that clear, Paris Beaufont?"

All eyes in the court cut to Paris. She didn't dare breathe or blink, and she was pretty sure her blood quit beating in her veins for a moment. Finally, she mustered the courage to mutter one clear word. "Infinitely."

CHAPTER FIFTY

I f having to be the mediator between the queen of the Seelie and the king of the Unseelie wasn't enough, now Paris had to apprehend the Knees and bring them to Queen Helena MacGillie. She had the run-in with Courtney and now the other one at Loose Teeth College, but like the cowards they were, they always fled. How was she going to catch three fairies? It felt like an overwhelming task, but it was the only way to get the Seelie queen to clean the Fang Wellspring. That had to happen for all the right reasons.

Before, cleaning the wellspring would ensure they got Headmistress Sham's support against the Knees. Now Paris had to go after them herself. Since realizing the positive repercussions of cleaning the Fang Wellspring, she knew she had to do it. It was full of dark magic that only created more problems.

If by cleaning it, the fairy godmothers and the tooth fairies could get along, and others would have a clean magic source, then that's what needed to happen. First, Paris had to find the three rebel fairies.

"Do you think Headmistress Sham will simply turn the Knees over to us?" Paris asked Headmistress Starr as they stepped through the vortex door back to the juniper forest—entering the realm of the fairy godmothers once more.

"That's my hope." Willow brushed off her blue gown, although it was still pristine. "I'll send her a message as soon as we return to Happily Ever After College."

"You're back!" Sophia exclaimed, popping up at the sight of them. She and Lunis appeared to be playing Tic-tac-toe in the dirt—her using a stick and him using his claw to draw.

"Oh, so you're back..." Lunis didn't sound as excited. "I guess that means I can't have your talking squirrel."

"Lun," Sophia complained, slapping her dragon on the side.

"What?" he argued. "He's so cool with his knowledge of science and squeaky voice, like a little rodent Albert Einstein. I had so many plans for us. Like, I was going to wait until he buried a nut and swap it for a grilled cheese sandwich when he wasn't looking. That would blow his mind."

"He'd love the sandwich," Paris admitted with a laugh. "But fat chance of getting Faraday to bury a nut. He's allergic."

Lunis groaned. "Oh, and it keeps getting worse. He's the best squirrel ever." He glanced at Sophia. "Please murder your niece so I can have her squirrel. I don't ask for much."

"You sort of do." Sophia giggled. "And no."

Lunis lowered his head so it was even with his rider's and eyed her intently. "I order you, Sophia Beaufont, to slay your niece. Do it!"

She laughed some more. "That still doesn't work. I've told you before that you don't have mind control over me."

The blue dragon shrugged. "Fine, it was worth a shot."

"You should protect Paris," Willow cut in. "Not only is she the key to saving the fairy godmothers, although the specifics on that are still unclear. We found out what was in the letter from Papa Creola."

"It was chain mail, wasn't it?" Lunis asked quite seriously.

Willow shook her head as if she also thought he was serious. "No, according to Papa Creola, Paris is the key to finally laying to rest the tension between the Seelie and the Unseelie. She appears to be the peacekeeper they've been waiting for."

"Sounds like a dangerous job," Lunis muttered. "Maybe she'll die in the process..."

"Lun," Sophia scolded.

"What?" he argued. "I need an eccentric squirrel. My hedgehog is boring."

"You're only going to get yourself in trouble if you have a squirrel as a pet," Sophia stated.

"Nope," he replied. "Squirrels are like cigarettes and completely harmless...well, unless you stick one in your mouth and light them on fire."

Paris laughed. "Sorry to disappoint, but I don't plan on dying."

"That is disappointing." The blue dragon draped his head solemnly. "If I had Faraday as a pet, we could come up with lots of nutty puns."

"Please stop," Sophia begged.

"Last one," Lunis sang. "Why did the squirrel fall out of the tree?"

"Why?" Sophia asked in a dry voice.

"Because it was dead," he answered with a roaring laugh.

Turning to Paris, Sophia said, "Would you like a dragon? I'm giving one away."

Paris shook her head. "No, thanks."

Resigning, Sophia shrugged. "Well, that's pretty incredible that you're the peacekeeper for the Seelie and the Unseelie. They've been fighting for ages."

Paris sighed. "Yes, but something tells me that it won't be easy and my success isn't guaranteed."

"I'm afraid not," Willow stated.

"When you do succeed, because I know you will, you'll get a Nobel Peace Prize," Sophia said proudly.

"Speaking of which," Lunis said casually. "Did you hear about the Irish farmer who won the Nobel Peace Prize?"

"No, I haven't," Willow said with interest because she apparently was too polite or hadn't caught on yet.

Lunis nodded. "Yeah, he was found outstanding in his field."

"On that note," Sophia sang, "I bet you two want a ride home."

Both Willow and Paris nodded.

"Yes, I'm beat after all these crazy adventures," Paris admitted.

"I have important matters to attend do," Willow added.

"Fine, I'll be your flying Uber." Lunis extended his wing, making a ramp for the three to climb onto his back. "I won't even entertain you with my comedy."

Paris stepped up, taking a seat on the blue dragon. "Well, I hoped you would tell a few more jokes."

"You did?" Sophia turned from her spot at the front in surprise.

"Well, that's better than his stories." Paris hid her laugh. "They tend to drag on…"

CHAPTER FIFTY-ONE

Trying to play at Lunis' own game and tell bad jokes didn't work. It only encouraged the dragon. He wasn't quiet for more than a few seconds, telling joke after joke on the flight back to Happily Ever After College. Paris was grateful for the distraction since she felt a heavy weight pushing her shoulders down from the pressures ahead.

On top of the graduation project, which was huge to begin with, she had to track down the Knees and help the Seelie and Unseelie get along when they hadn't in so long. She planned to visit Papa Creola and find out more details, not that he would supply them. She didn't want to enter into this whole mess blindly. However, she was aware that Queen Helena MacGillie would be watching her somehow at all times, looking for signs that she wasn't going to comply.

If Paris wasn't intimidated before, she was now.

When Lunis let Willow and her off on the Enchanted Grounds of Happily Ever After College, relief flooded Paris' chest. It was late—the adventures had taken them away for most of the day. Night had set at the college, and the mansion in the distance was dark, many of the staff and students asleep.

Paris couldn't wait to join them. Then the next day she could wake up and hopefully approach the challenges ahead with a clear head.

Things had to look less intimidating after a long night's rest and some advice and a pep talk from Faraday.

Willow and Paris waved at Sophia and Lunis as they glided through the portal, leaving Happily Ever After College. When they were gone, and the portal closed, the pair turned back to the mansion, setting off for the front door.

They hadn't taken two steps when a blood-curdling scream shot through the air—its origin without a doubt coming from the darkened house in front of them.

CHAPTER FIFTY-TWO

Paris froze. So did Willow. Paris' horrified look reflected in the fairy godmother's eyes.

Without saying a word, both seemed to know what happened next. As a subsequent scream rang through the air, Paris launched forward, instantly sprinting. Willow followed but couldn't keep up since Paris had the speed lent to her from her demon blood. She was across the Enchanted Grounds and had cleared the steps of the patio within seconds.

Glancing over her shoulder, she noted that the fairy godmother was still some distance away. Paris didn't think that waiting for her would do any good. Something was wrong at Happily Ever After College. When it came to danger, Paris was the fairy most prepared to deal with it.

Without hesitating, Paris opened the front door and swung it back, standing ready for whatever she found on the other side—inside the usually cheery and warm mansion. What Paris saw next, she never would've expected in a hundred years.

The fairy godmother estate was unlike she ever could've imagined. For a moment, Paris second-guessed if they were at the right location. It felt more like this was the mansion at Loose Teeth College.

The mansion of Happily Ever After College appeared to be haunted.

CHAPTER FIFTY-THREE

Mirrors hung in the long hallway that ran along the entrance of the mansion. Large reflective surfaces of various sizes also lined the stairs leading up to the second floor. To Paris' horror, it appeared that blood was dripping down the surface of each mirror.

Like the house of Loose Teeth College, the mansion was dark, as if all the lights had suddenly burned out. The only illumination was from candles. However, they weren't in holders or candelabras. Strangely, the white candlesticks floated in the air on either side of each mirror.

Knowing that it would be unwise to rush into the mansion when it was so different, Paris was still at the threshold when Willow finally arrived, having been surveying the entryway. The halfling knew she'd be no use to anyone if she rushed into the house and got herself killed by whatever was suddenly terrorizing the college.

The headmistress' eyes widened at the sight in front of them, also not rushing forward. She gasped. All color drained from her face. Paris glanced from the sight around them and back to Willow.

"What is it?" Paris whispered.

Willow appeared to have trouble breathing for a moment. Finally, she choked out a breath, and her voice was scratchy when she answered. "Bloody Mary."

CHAPTER FIFTY-FOUR

"Zora Tali." Paris thought of the new student trying to recruit students to do the Bloody Mary ritual with her. Chef Ash had said that it would be impossible for her to assimilate everything she needed to make it happen, but it appeared that he was wrong, and she'd been successful. Still, why would the magician want to do this? The chilly air and sounds of screaming on the mansion's second floor told Paris that Bloody Mary was a really bad thing.

Willow nodded.

All that Paris had known about Bloody Mary was what she'd recently learned. She was an evil spirit, which if conjured, came out of a mirror and stole people away, killed them, or stole their soul. None of that worked for Paris. She was instantly madder than hell.

"How do we get rid of Bloody Mary?" She still didn't dare to enter the mansion without having the proper knowledge to defend herself. She reasoned that she was safe until she crossed the threshold.

Willow gave her a regretful look. "I don't know. Bloody Mary is dark magic, and that's not something I know anything about."

Paris chewed on her lip, thinking. She needed information, and although she knew how to get it, that would require a risk. Holding her breath, she made an impromptu decision. Taking a step forward,

Paris crossed the threshold, saying four quick words before she jumped back out of the mansion.

"Wilfred, I need you!"

A moment later, the magitech AI appeared on the other side of the threshold. Although the refined butler always appeared the same, relaxed and polished, he suddenly seemed very worried—horror covering his gaze.

CHAPTER FIFTY-FIVE

W illow sighed at the sight of her trusty butler, relief covering her gaze.

"Good thinking, Paris." She nodded at her before glancing back at Wilfred. "What's going on? Are the students okay?"

He shook his head of gray hair. "I'm afraid they aren't. I've been trying to communicate to them how to survive the ghost of Bloody Mary until we can get rid of her."

"How do we get rid of her?" Willow asked, and in quick succession, she sputtered, "How do they survive her?"

"I don't know the answer to the first question." Regret lay heavy in Wilfred's tone. "To survive her, Penny said that no one was to look into the mirrors. If you do, you'll see Bloody Mary, and she'll come through."

"Tell all the students to leave," Paris ordered. "Then they'll be on the grounds of the college and safe. Chef Ash and Christine said that if Bloody Mary doesn't have anyone to feast upon, she loses energy and it forces her to retreat to where she came from."

He shook his head. "There has been a curse placed on the mansion. All those who were inside it during Bloody Mary's summoning can't leave. We're trapped."

Paris groaned. She wasn't inside the mansion for the ritual so she could cross the threshold and back. However, all her friends...all of the students...the staff were trapped inside the mansion with a deadly ghost.

"It was Zora Tali who did this, wasn't it?" Paris asked, anger heavy in her voice.

Wilfred nodded at once. "According to Casanova, she was able to assemble the right number of students to help her to conjure the ghost of Bloody Mary."

The tattle cat was finally good for something, Paris thought, remembering that the orange cat usually spied on students and reported their bad behavior to Willow. "She had all the artifacts too? Chef Ash didn't think that was likely."

"Apparently," Wilfred stated. "There's something else of importance I think you should know if you enter the mansion."

"We're entering the house," Paris argued. "We have to help you all."

Willow nodded. "Yes, of course. What is it we need to know?"

"It's about Zora Tali," he answered. "She won't look the same as when you saw her."

"Why?" Willow asked in a rush.

"She took off the blue gown," Paris guessed.

"Yes, that," Wilfred replied. "Also, she was wearing a disguise before. Not anymore though. From what I've been able to deduce, she's not Zora Tali at all. Based on facial recognition and matching it to a worldwide Internet database, I believe her name is Whitney Ives."

"Whitney..." Paris said, the true implications dawning.

Willow gasped. "Then that would mean..."

Paris completed the headmistress' sentence. "She's one of the Knees from Loose Teeth College."

CHAPTER FIFTY-SIX

"I allowed a tooth fairy into Happily Ever After College," Willow said, regret heavy in her voice. She was already guilting herself for what had happened.

"It's not your fault," Paris stated. "Let's look at the bright side. If Whitney cursed all of the students not to be able to leave the mansion, it should keep her trapped inside there too. We have to get rid of Bloody Mary and capture Whitney. Then we'll be that much closer to fulfilling what Queen Helena MacGillie asked for."

Willow nodded but didn't appear encouraged by the information.

It made sense that Whitney was the Knee sent to do this type of spell work on the mansion. Only a magician would be able to pull off such a complex ritual and a trapping spell. The bad news that Paris didn't want to tell Willow was, although the curse would keep Whitney inside the mansion, she could also take it down and escape. However, if she did that, the students would be free from Bloody Mary too. So it was almost a blessing if Whitney got scared, took down the spell, and fled.

Paris glanced around inside the darkened and foreboding hallway on the other side of Wilfred with its bloody mirrors and floating candles. Somewhere inside the mansion was the evil tooth fairy Paris needed to apprehend. However, also inside the house were all her friends and innocent fairies who needed her help.

She turned to Willow with conviction in her gaze. "We have to find out how to get rid of Bloody Mary. That's the only way to save those trapped inside."

"I realize that," Willow said, tears in her voice. "I don't know how, though."

"That's where I can help," a familiar voice said at their back.

Paris and Willow turned to find the unassuming form of Mae Ling standing on the porch behind them—a glint of determination in her small brown eyes.

CHAPTER FIFTY-SEVEN

"Mae Ling." Willow looked the other fairy over. "Are you okay?" She nodded.

"You weren't inside the mansion when the trapping spell happened?" Willow asked.

"I was in the greenhouse with Hemingway," she answered.

"What a relief," Willow stated.

"How do we get rid of Bloody Mary?" Paris was conscious of the sounds of crying and faint screams coming from inside the mansion.

"It won't be easy," Mae Ling answered.

"It never is," Paris muttered. "What does it involve?"

"A reverse ritual that banishes the ghost," Mae Ling explained.

"You know how to do this?" Willow asked in a rush.

The other fairy nodded. "I'll need help. Willow, I'll need you to accompany me to the attic. We have to draw the diagram on the top floor of the house where Whitney conjured Bloody Mary."

Willow shivered, obviously not loving the idea of entering the haunted mansion filled with mirrors. That must have been a part of Whitney's doing, knowing that the more mirrors present, the more dangerous the ghost would be. It appeared that the Knees were out for blood if they'd gone to these lengths to destroy Happily Ever After

College. "Okay. I'll do that. Then what? We do a reverse ritual, and Bloody Mary is gone? How long will that take?"

"Not long," Mae Ling answered. "However, it's a bit more complicated than that. Besides the diagram we must draw and the spells we need to perform, we need three things to complete the reverse ritual." The small woman looked intently at Paris. "That's where I'll need your help. Can you retrieve things from inside the mansion and meet us in the attic?"

"Of course," Paris stated. "What do you need?"

Mae Ling gave her a warning look. "Only three simple things, but getting them without running into Bloody Mary will be the tricky part."

CHAPTER FIFTY-EIGHT

Wilfred had told most of the women in the fairy godmother mansion to hide or stay away from mirrors. That meant that besides the initial attacks, which Paris didn't want to think about, most of the students and staff were safe for the time being. As long as they didn't look directly into any of the hundreds of mirrors placed inside the building, they would be okay.

However, they needed to perform the reverse ritual right away. According to Casanova, who was spying on Whitney hiding in a closet on the second floor, she was willing to resort to desperate measures to get the students out of their hiding places so they met Bloody Mary. The idea of marching up to that closet, yanking the evil tooth fairy from her spot, and shoving her face in front of a mirror tempted Paris.

However, that wouldn't help to save those trapped inside the mansion. Her first goal had to be to protect them. Then she'd cart Whitney off to Queen Helena MacGillie—who would surely deliver a worse fate than Paris could give her. She reasoned, why get her hands dirty with the magician's blood if she could let the Seelie queen do it?

The job Mae Ling had assigned to Paris was dangerous because traveling through the mansion without meeting Bloody Mary would be difficult. It was almost impossible to go to all the three different places she needed to without looking into one of the many mirrors hanging on the walls. The objects Paris needed to retrieve wouldn't be hard to find. However, they happened to be at opposite parts of the mansion, meaning Paris would have to cover a lot of ground—and fast.

She considered opening a portal and getting the objects from somewhere else. However, Mae Ling had stated that she didn't think portals would open back into Happily Ever After College from the outside. The trapping spell locked the students and staff inside the mansion and locked anyone not already on the grounds out, keeping them from entering.

It was a very advanced spell that was a direct result of dark magic from the Fang Wellspring. This further fueled Paris' reasoning that she needed to do whatever it took to have Queen Helena MacGillie clean that source of dirty magic.

The advanced locking spell meant that Paris couldn't leave, and it also meant that they couldn't call for backup. The fairy godmothers were on their own. It was up to Willow, Mae Ling, and Paris to get rid of Bloody Mary and capture the evil tooth fairy. Hopefully, they could do it fast before anyone else was hurt or stolen away by the angry spirit.

"Are you ready to do this?" Mae Ling asked Paris, having run through the list only once.

She nodded. "The kitchen. The conservatory. Faraday's lab. Then meet you two in the attic. I can do it."

"I know you can." The ancient wisdom that Mae Ling exuded radiated from her piercing gaze.

"You two will be able to get to the attic safely?" Paris asked, worried for the two fairy godmothers.

"Fortunately for us, all we have to do is make it up to the attic." Mae Ling indicated herself and Willow. "That means we can close our eyes and make the trek."

Willow nodded. "I know the mansion well enough that I can find my way up to the attic blindfolded."

"Unfortunately for you," Mae Ling began, regret in her voice. "The items you need to locate will require that you search a bit, which means you'll need to look around. Keep your eyes low. If you do look at a mirror and pull Bloody Mary through, do the only thing that will keep you alive."

Paris' heart beat so hard in her chest that she felt the pulsing in her throat. "What's that?"

The chill in Mae Ling's eyes sent a shiver down Paris' back like it was suddenly winter on the grounds. "Run like hell."

CHAPTER FIFTY-NINE

Wilfred would've been a great help to Paris in retrieving her objects. However, he was best suited to ensure that all the students stayed hidden and to keep an eye on Whitney. There were only so many versions of the AI, and the number of current students with increased enrollment far outnumbered him.

Also, Paris thought that if Wilfred was going to lead anyone through the mansion, it needed to be Willow and Mae Ling up to the attic. If something did happen to Paris, the two women would redirect Wilfred to pick up where she left off. However, Mae Ling had an unwavering conviction in Paris' ability to pull this off. The halfling wasn't sure why the fairy godmother had such faith in her, but she had from the beginning. More than ever, Paris didn't want to let her down.

From the other side of the threshold, Paris watched as Willow and Mae Ling stepped into the fairy godmother mansion hand-in-hand. Wilfred was beside them in the entryway, there to give them directions if they went off-course with their eyes closed. As long as they traversed the three flights of stairs without looking in a mirror— meaning they kept their eyes shut—they would be okay.

They weren't entirely out of danger then. Once in the attic, they needed to draw the diagram for the reverse ritual on the floor and perform the spell. That part would require opening their eyes. However, that's where Wilfred would be most important to them.

The magitech AI butler was to find a spot in the attic that didn't have mirrors stationed around. Much like the trapping spell that kept the fairies locked inside the mansion, a spell on the mirrors kept them glued to the wall. It appeared that the rotten Knees had thought of everything.

Paris gritted her teeth, undeterred. It would take more than a stupid evil spirit to defeat her. Not only did she intend to find the three necessary objects to complete the reverse ritual, but she'd deliver them to Mae Ling and Willow in record time. As soon as the coast was clear, Paris would find the magician tooth fairy known as Whitney and break her pretty little nose. That way, when she met Queen Helena MacGillie, she looked especially offensive. The Seelie queen would no doubt be angry when forced to look at someone who had broken laws as well as looked repulsive.

Once Willow and Mae Ling were out of sight, it was Paris' turn to enter the house. The first and closest place she needed to visit was the kitchen. Thankfully for the first trek of her mission, like the fairy godmothers, she could keep her eyes closed up until she arrived there. Unfortunately, she'd have to open her eyes to find the object. After she retrieved it, her eyes would have to remain open most of the time.

Paris sucked in a breath and closed her eyes as she picked up her foot and took a step into the haunted mansion of Happily Ever After.

CHAPTER SIXTY

The chill that wrapped around Paris was instant. She suddenly felt like she'd been transported back onto the grounds of Loose Teeth College. Adding to the foreboding atmosphere, plus the fact that Paris was walking down the long corridor toward the back of the mansion with her eyes closed, there was a soft howling sound. That had to be Bloody Mary haunting from the mirrors, Paris reasoned.

She didn't want to think about how many students or staff members looked into the mirrors before Wilfred had spread the warning to hide. Her heart hurt for any who had suffered that night and were irreversibly taken and gone.

However, Paris could only imagine how the howling was haunting those who had their heads buried and were trying not to look around. It chilled Paris to the bone. It made her want to run—to get as far from the haunting sound as possible. Yet, as with the boogeyman, the only way to stay safe was to close one's eyes and hide. Looking under one's bed would only bring the monster out.

Life was stupidly ironic. Paris held out her hand, running her fingers along the wall's surface. When the tips knocked against a mirror, she sucked in a breath, hoping that touching the mirror didn't bring Bloody Mary out.

However, she'd progressed quite far, nearly to the kitchen without getting the impression that she'd drawn the ghost from her spot. Apparently, looking into a mirror in a house where someone had conjured Bloody Mary was the only way she could attack. They would immediately see the ghost behind them. Then when they turned, she would be there in physical form, and the chase would begin.

Paris hoped not to see the ghost in real life—or otherwise. She also wished not to have to outrun her. If all went well, she'd retrieve the objects she needed and get them to Willow and Mae Ling as soon as they finished with the diagram and were ready for them.

Running through the layout of the kitchen, Paris tried to recall where the serrated knives would be. Chef Ash was very organized with his kitchen utensils, which should make them easier to find. However, not even the kitchen had been spared of mirrors when Whitney did her voodoo, according to Wilfred. Therefore, Paris would have to be careful.

She hadn't asked why one of the three objects for the reverse ritual was a serrated knife. Paris knew better than to question Mae Ling. However, when she entered the room that smelled of sauteed onions and spices, she wished that the fairy godmother had told her if she could use the knife to stab someone.

That was her thought as a metal frying pan whacked her across the head, knocked her to the floor, and sent her to a world of total blackness...darker than how things had been when she'd had her eyes closed.

CHAPTER SIXTY-ONE

Paris' head was pounding, and she was pretty sure it was bleeding too. Her biggest concern was that she was awake and lying flat on her back somewhere in the fairy godmother mansion and unable to open her eyes and kill whoever had attacked her.

"Oh dear, the angels," a familiar voice said in hushed tones. "It's Paris."

"I know," Chef Ash said in a rush. "She's bleeding."

"I think she's unconscious. Do you think we killed her?"

Paris groaned and dared to open her eyes, guessing if these two dorks were standing over her, it was safe to look around.

"She's not dead," Chef Ash said with relief as Paris made to push up.

"But you two are about to be," Paris said in a slurred voice, opening her eyes to find Chef Ash and Christine crouched in front of her in the kitchen.

"Oh, good, you're all right," Christine said with relief.

"That's a matter of opinion," Paris complained, hunching over to feel the back of her head. She was bleeding, and the open wound felt gross. Pulling her hand away, she decided that she'd tend to that later when her friends weren't attacking her, and an evil spirit wasn't loose in the fairy godmother mansion.

"You've got quite the gash back there," Chef Ash said, remorse in his tone as he handed her a clean dish rag from a nearby counter. "I can wrap it up if you'd like."

Paris shook her head, regretting it immediately. "I'll be okay. I'm more concerned why you two dimwits hit me with a frying pan. Then my next concern is how I'm going to kill you. Then my third one is who goes first."

Now that her eyes were open, Paris could see that although seeming to lack reason, having attacked her with a frying pan, the kitchen appeared to be a safe place. All of the mirrors had something non-reflective covering them, like pots or pans or lids. She sighed a breath of relief.

"I'm so sorry, Paris," Christine began. "It was dark, and we were hiding in here, as Wilfred told us to do. Then you entered, but all we saw was the outline of your figure. So I grabbed a frying pan and hit you across the head with it. I'm sorry. I thought you were Bloody Mary."

Paris rolled her eyes, the small gesture registering in her sore head. "So you thought you could whack Bloody Mary? She's a ghost, you know?"

"I know." Christine scrunched up her nose. "I panicked."

Even in the dark of the kitchen, Paris could see the regret in her friend's eyes and softened. "It's okay. Things are crazy here right now. I'm glad you two are okay."

"We're fine," Chef Ash stated. "We made it safe in here as soon as we figured out what was happening. I nearly pulled Blood Mary through, but thankfully I got the mirrors covered before it could happen."

"Good thinking." Paris was grateful she could look around freely.

"What are you doing here?" Christine asked. "Wilfred said we were to stay put until Bloody Mary was gone and soon help would be on the way."

"I'm help," Paris remarked dryly, pushing up to her feet and looking around. "Headmistress Starr and Mae Ling sent me to recover what they need to banish the evil spirit. Chef Ash, can I get a serrated knife, please?"

"I said I was sorry," Christine said at once, holding up her hands and backing away suddenly.

Paris chuckled. "I'm not going to stab you...yet. It's one of the objects they sent me for. They're doing a reverse ritual to get rid of Bloody Mary."

Chef Ash nodded as if this made sense, then turned away to a worktop and looked around. "I'm glad someone knows that. I was hoping..."

"Do you need our help finding these objects?" Christine asked. "I'll do whatever you need."

Chef Ash agreed to the participation with a nod, turning back and handing Paris a serrated knife with a long blade. "Yeah, what else do you need?"

She took it. "Thanks, but I think this is better as a one-person job. You two are safe in here, and there needs to be backup if something happens to me. Hopefully, I can be fast, and they can complete the reverse ritual."

Christine sighed. "I hope so. It was super creepy when we all came out of the dining hall, and the lights went out, mirrors were everywhere, and floating candles. No one knew what was happening. It soon turned to complete chaos, and everyone went running."

Paris shivered, imagining the whole thing. "That sounds awful. Were many people hurt?"

Chef Ash shrugged. "It's hard to say. I saw Bloody Mary snatch a few people before I grabbed Christine and we hid in here, after covering the mirrors, of course."

"Good thinking." Regret welling up in Paris' being at the thought that the spirit had snatched people. It sounded like it all happened fast and was terrifying.

Bolstering her courage, Paris held the handle of the serrated knife tightly in her hand. "Okay, well, you two stay here and safe. I'm going back out there to get what else they need for the reverse ritual."

They both nodded, fear evident in their eyes.

"Be safe," Chef Ash cautioned with an edge of tension in his voice.

"Let us know if you need our help," Christine added.

"Thanks." Paris made for the exit. "Stop hitting innocent people with frying pans, you weirdos."

CHAPTER SIXTY-TWO

Holding a knife and walking through a darkened, haunted hallway with one's eyes closed wasn't a smart idea, so Paris had to risk it and keep them open. She craned her aching head downward, looking straight at the floor as she progressed toward the conservatory.

Thankfully, she could make out where she was heading for the most part since the reflections of the mirrors weren't visible in her line of sight. Still, Paris couldn't see what was up ahead. She could be walking straight into danger for all she knew.

The next item she needed was cilantro, which grew in pots in the conservatory because it needed full sun. Chef Ash kept it there because it was close for him to access when cooking and it wouldn't thrive if he had it in the kitchen. That was good for Paris since she didn't want to have to go too far and risk looking in a mirror, but it still felt like the longest trek she'd ever taken in the mansion.

Similar to when Paris entered the kitchen, she knew when she approached the conservatory because of the familiar smell of herbs that lined the floor-to-ceiling glass windows. She also noticed the lack of light ahead and wondered why. The candles next to the mirrors eerily lit the hallway. Paris guessed that Whitney had cut the power throughout the mansion to make things more difficult for everyone.

With her head down and eyes on her feet, Paris was grateful that her shoulder-length hair framed her face, covering her peripheral vision. However, that meant she would have to use her memory to find the cilantro. She thought it was in the corner of the conservatory. If she could make her way straight over to it, she could nip as much as Willow and Mae Ling needed for the reverse ritual and be off.

The last thing she wanted to do was look up where she could potentially look into a mirror. Then she'd have to run like hell for the exit. Thankfully it wasn't far since the conservatory was at the back of the mansion. However, Paris didn't know how fast Bloody Mary was...and she didn't want to find out.

Paris carefully stepped toward the corner. Then someone came up behind her and clapped a hand over her eyes.

"What are you doing here?" someone whispered in her ear, his breath hot.

CHAPTER SIXTY-THREE

Tensing, her hand on the serrated knife handle, Paris clenched her eyes shut under Hemingway's hand pressed to her face. She knew he was the one holding her from behind—she recognized his scent—earth and wood. She'd recognize his voice anywhere, although it was a tense whisper. The way he pressed against her, well, Paris knew the way he felt although the occasions hadn't been numerous.

Hemingway didn't know that Paris had a head injury. Otherwise, he probably wouldn't have her head pressed against him so tightly or his hand over her eyes. He evidently thought she was taking a nightly stroll, looking for a snack in the conservatory.

Gripping the hand clasped to her face, she held it. "I'm getting things for Mae Ling. She knows how to do the reverse ritual to get rid of Bloody Mary."

He sighed with relief. "Oh, good, she figured it out. She said that she'd have to look it up in her notes."

"She got up to her room on the third floor and down again?" Paris was impressed. "That woman is incredible."

"She climbed the side of the mansion," Hemingway said, his hand still over her eyes, blocking her vision. Paris felt his head pressed against her as if he was holding her for comfort rather than protection.

"What are you doing here?" Paris asked. "Mae Ling said you two were in the greenhouse when this started. It's not worth risking being in here when you're not trapped in the mansion."

"I know," he stated. "But I was hanging directly outside the conservatory, keeping watch the best I could when I saw you entering the room. I knew you weren't here when this started and thought you might need a warning."

"Wow, you got in here soundlessly. I didn't hear you."

She felt him smile against her head. "I'm a ninja."

"No, you're not," Paris said with a smile too. "So I appreciate you trying to protect me, but I need to round up some cilantro for Mae Ling's reverse ritual. Can you point me in the direction? I'm trying to avoid looking up to see mirrors."

"There are no mirrors in here," Hemingway explained.

"Oh, that's good news."

"Not really," he countered. "The glass walls serve as reflections."

"Oh." Paris gulped as the realization dawned on her. "So the entire room is one big mirror."

"Exactly," he stated. "Which was why I knew I had to stop you. Unfortunately, when this started, and I ran for the conservatory, I saw a student trying to flee. She didn't make it out."

Paris shivered. "So you saw Bloody Mary then…"

"I didn't," Hemingway corrected. "I think you only see her if you see her in a mirrored surface. But I did see the fairy disappear. She was there one moment, then gone."

Paris bit down on her lip. "Where does she take them?"

"I don't know," he said darkly. "But I'm fairly certain there's no way to get them back."

"Well, we can figure that out later," Paris said, sighing away the stress of the moment. She needed to focus. "I have to get the cilantro."

"Yes, and the knife must be for Mae Ling's reverse ritual too?"

Paris nodded, her head still in his grasp.

"Okay, well, wait here, and I'll get it," Hemingway ordered. "But keep your eyes closed when I pull my arm away."

"No!" Paris exclaimed, but it was too late. Hemingway released her quickly and was gone from behind her. She clenched her eyes shut, biting on her lip again, this time from frustration.

"I know where it is," he stated. "You'll be fumbling around for ages trying to find it."

"I don't fumble around," Paris argued, making him laugh although the circumstances were so awful.

"No, you're as graceful as a ballerina." He chuckled.

"Okay, that's almost worse, calling me a ballerina," she joked. "I've changed my mind. I fumble."

Soundlessly Hemingway arrived by her side again, pressing a bunch of soft green herbs into her free hand. "Here you go. Now, what do you need next?"

Sensing that he was right in front of her, Paris looked up, her eyes closed. She felt his breath on her and enjoyed it despite the stress of the situation.

"I've got to go to Faraday's lab," she explained.

"I'll go with you," he insisted.

Paris shook her head but realizing he would have his head down and hopefully, his eyes closed, she said, "No, it's safer for only one of us to go. You can leave, so keep watch from outside the conservatory again. I can make it."

"His lab is on the far side of the mansion on the third floor," Hemingway argued. "Are you sure you need to go all the way there?"

"Do you know another place in the mansion that has thirty feet of underground armored feeder cables?" Paris asked, her eyes still closed and chin held up like she was looking directly at Hemingway.

"Yeah, you have to go to Faraday's lab," he said with regret. "Too bad there isn't a window in his lab."

"Yeah, the dork didn't want one because he said he's allergic to the outdoors," Paris joked. "And that the sunlight would interfere with his nerdy experiments."

A thought suddenly occurred to Paris. "Hey, but I could climb up to the third floor the same way as Mae Ling."

"Good idea," he stated. "Then you can climb through a nearby window and get into the lab."

Paris shoved the herbs into the pocket of her leather jacket but held onto the knife. She'd have to climb with it in her hand.

Hemingway felt around for her hand and tugged her for the door. "Come on. I'll supervise you from the ground. Keep your eyes closed until you feel the night air on your face."

Paris did as he told her, grateful that she wasn't alone for all of this. She also hoped that Faraday was safe in his lab. She'd need his help to find the cable or she'd be delayed for a while trying to find it.

CHAPTER SIXTY-FOUR

The night air was such a welcome relief, making Paris feel instantly warmer after being in the frigid mansion. Part of her wanted to run as far from the haunted house as possible, leaving all her troubles behind. However, she knew that was impossible. Not only could she not leave everyone trapped, but her troubles would also follow her one way or another if she knew that others were in danger.

"Okay, can you climb up the drainage pipe on the corner of the mansion?" Hemingway asked, pointing at the side of the darkened house.

Paris scoffed at him. "Where did you first meet me?"

He chuckled. "I believe you were in a tree."

"Exactly," Paris said proudly. "Yes, I'll use the lattice on either side for foot and handholds."

"Good," he affirmed. "I think the corner is the best bet because you don't want to risk looking through a window on the side and seeing a mirror."

"But I'm outside the mansion," she argued.

Hemingway shrugged. "Let's not risk it. The key is going to be reentering on the third floor."

She pointed to the first window closest to the corner on the eastern side of the mansion. "That one is nearest to Faraday's lab. I'll crawl through there, stay on my hands and knees and make my way to his door. Let's hope that it's unlocked or I'm turning that squirrel into a purse."

Hemingway laughed. "I can't see you carrying a purse if I'm honest."

"It's entertaining that was your takeaway from my threat."

"Does Faraday ever get tired of your threats?"

"He loves them." Paris headed for the corner of the mansion, hiking up her leg to start the long climb, which she hoped to make short work of.

"Okay, well be careful, Pare. I need you back."

She glanced over her shoulder, her hands reaching up over her head. "I have every intention of returning to you."

CHAPTER SIXTY-FIVE

Paris had once learned that falling from nine feet or below was the safest height to avoid serious injury. Anything above that could result in broken bones or worse. She also knew that the third story of a house was roughly forty-five feet tall. Before she cleared the first story, she'd already be at a dangerous height.

"Don't look down," Paris muttered to herself.

"You're doing great," Hemingway encouraged from the ground.

"Thanks," Paris replied through gritted teeth, finding it increasingly harder to climb with the handle of the serrated knife in her hand. Her heart was already wildly beating once she was past the first set of windows, but that was more from the adrenaline than the strain of the exercise.

However, once she was nearly past the second story, her muscles were beginning to ache. That's when Paris remembered that she'd already had two big adventures before this—and no rest or food. She was exhausted, but she'd have to get over it.

Looking up, Paris was grateful to see that the window she needed to climb through wasn't far ahead. Sadly, no windows led into the attic, so she'd have to walk through the third floor to get there.

Although holding the knife was making the climb harder, catching sight of the reflective sight of the blade gave Paris an idea. She thought that she was okay being outside the house. It was possible that if she looked directly into a mirror on the other side of the window and saw Bloody Mary that she'd be inside the mansion waiting for her—ready to attack when she entered. Still, if she could avoid angling the blade to catch a mirror and didn't linger for a long look, being outside the spell might not trigger the ghost.

When Paris made it to the third-story window, she traversed directly underneath it. Then she held up the blade of the serrated knife, using the indirect glimpse to show her what was on the other side of the window. She was outside Faraday's lab at the main hallway.

The reflection from the knife told her that mirrors lined the wood-paneled hallway. However, they didn't start for a few feet from the window. If she kept her eyes low as she climbed through, she could avoid looking into one of them. Paris pulled the knife down, gripped the lattice, and used her other hand to wiggle the window open. Thankfully it slid up without issue.

Looking over her shoulder, Paris gave Hemingway one last look. He glanced up at her—worry heavy in his eyes. Tenderly, he kissed his hand and blew her a kiss. She smiled and kissed the air, the gesture intended for him, although her hands were full and she couldn't blow it down to him. Then without another moment of delay, Paris climbed the rest of the way over the side of the window back into the haunted mansion.

She was careful to keep her eyes low to not look into a mirror and pull Bloody Mary through.

CHAPTER SIXTY-SIX

On her hands and knees, Paris progressed to the first door. Unlike all the rest of the doors in the fairy godmother mansion, the one that led to Faraday's lab was a metal push door. It was safer and more conducive for his science experiments than the wood ones with the elegant crown molding.

The distant howling Paris had heard before echoed down the hallway, making her tense as she lifted her hand for the metal knob. Silently, Paris prayed that Faraday's lab was open. She held her breath as she pressed down on the handle. It caught instantly, telling her that he'd locked it.

Paris banged her forehead against the metal surface in frustration, but that only made her injured head feel worse.

"Damn it, Faraday," Paris groaned, wondering if the squirrel was asleep in her sock drawer on the second floor. He often locked his lab at night so no unsuspecting student strode into it and got themselves into trouble with one of his experiments.

"Pare!" the talking squirrel squealed on the other side of the door.

Paris' heart skipped, and she nearly looked up completely from the sudden excitement, but thankfully she remembered to keep her eyes on the floor. Behind the door was a *click* and a moment later, it swung back a few feet, showing a curious squirrel looking back at her with glasses around his eyes.

"Get in here!" he squeaked, waving her into his lab. "It's not safe out there! Haven't you heard that someone conjured Bloody Mary?"

Crawling on her hands and knees, with a knife in her hand, Paris hurried into the lab. As soon as she was through, Faraday closed the door behind her. She kept her eyes on the floor, not sure where the mirrors were in the lab.

"It's safe in here," he stated. "Because of the scientific wards I have on the place, they couldn't put mirrors in my lab. Plus, I've covered up anything reflective like the metal tool case and aluminum beakers."

Paris let out a breath and glanced up. Her neck was grateful for the relief of not looking down. "Yes, I'm aware that Bloody Mary is on the loose. Why do you think I'm crawling around with a knife in the middle of the night?"

He shrugged. "You do a lot of strange things that I don't question."

"I don't either." Paris stood tall, grateful to be able to look around freely. "So I need thirty feet of underground armored feeder cable and pronto."

Faraday nodded. "Case and point."

She snapped her fingers. "Did you hear the part where I said, pronto?"

"I'm on it." Instantly, he scurried for a cabinet, opened it, and disappeared.

Paris took this opportunity while he was rummaging through the storage area to draw a few breaths. "I'm glad you're safe."

"Same to you," he called in a muffled voice. "I knew you were gone and was grateful for that."

"And those glasses you're wearing?" Paris asked.

"They turn reflective surfaces into negative space," Faraday answered.

"Smart," she chirped. "I'll take a pair."

"I just fashioned these, and I don't think they'll fit you." A canister of what sounded like screws flew out of the open cabinet along with some random tools as the squirrel continued to dig around.

"How long until you can fashion some that fit me?" Paris asked.

"Probably longer than you have based on your order to be 'pronto.' Why do you need this cable?"

"To do a reverse ritual to send Blood Mary back to the hell pit she crawled from."

"That would also be why you're carrying a knife too?"

"And I have a pocket full of cilantro," Paris bragged.

"This sounds like a weird reverse ritual." Faraday surfaced with his fur all disheveled. In his paws, he had the end of a cable. "I have what you want. Grab this and tug. Then we'll twirl up the amount you need. Where are we headed to?"

"We aren't heading anywhere." Paris grabbed the cable and winding it up. "I'm not endangering your life when you're perfectly safe here. This is my quest."

"I have the glasses," he argued. "Plus, when have I ever not wanted to go on a quest with you? If you're in danger, I want to be too."

"That's kind of a sick mentality, but it's also heartwarming."

He pointed at the glasses. "I can be your eyes. I'll tell you where to go and help you get there."

Getting up to the attic with her head down or her eyes closed was going to be tough since she'd never been up there. Paris sighed and resigned herself to the squirrel's good sense. "Okay, fine. We need to get up to the attic and fast. Lead the way, Faraday. You'll be my eyes."

He scurried for the door, his tail waving like a flag behind him. "Pronto, Paris!"

CHAPTER SIXTY-SEVEN

With her eyes tightly pressed shut, Paris entered the hallway, the cold greeting her rudely once more along with the low howling of Bloody Mary in the distance.

"Okay, keep your eyes closed no matter what," Faraday called from beside her.

"Yeah, I've been playing this game all night. I know the rules," she joked.

"Mirrors line both sides of the hallway," he continued, not appreciating her joke. "The attic stairs are at the far end of this corridor, on the opposite side of the mansion."

"Of course they are," she grumbled, taking careful steps, feeling the carpet runner under her boots.

"It's a narrower staircase with a lower ceiling than the ones between the main floors," Faraday explained. "So you're going to need to duck for clearance."

"I've already been banged in the head tonight so it's cool if I lose a few more brain cells," Paris commented.

"Sounds like you've met some meanies." His claws made scratching sounds on the floor as he progressed next to her. He must've been on the wood beside the carpet runner.

"I met one of my friends," Paris explained. "They mistook me for an angry soul-eating witch and attacked me with a frying pan."

"That makes sense. Okay, in approximately sixteen inches, you'll need to step over a fallen table in the middle of the hallway."

"Oh, really?" Paris paused, realizing that there would be things strewn around from fleeing students. "Can you be a bit more specific on the distance?"

He *harrumphed*. "Edge forward until your boot connects with the table. It's two feet wide so you'll need to lift your leg that much to crawl around it."

Paris did as instructed, and a moment later, her shoe knocked into something hard. Leaning down, she felt around for parts of the table, trying to decide how to best get over the fallen object. She was instantly grateful that Faraday was guiding her. Otherwise, she would've run into the table and had a heck of a time trying to get through the obstacles.

When she was fairly certain that she'd cleared it, Paris stood tall once more. "Okay, now what?"

"Veer to the right to avoid tripping over a large vase that's lying in the middle of the corridor."

"Copy that," Paris replied, stepping to the far right side. She instantly felt the warmth from the firelight and made a note not to get too close to it.

After a few paces, Faraday said, "Okay, you're past it now."

"Good," Paris chirped. "How much farther to this staircase?"

"Not far," he stated. "Although there's one last obstacle, you can't walk around it."

"What is it?" Paris halted.

"There's broken glass from a fallen chandelier. You can veer to the left to avoid the main part of it, but you'll be walking over the glass and broken crystals. I want you to be aware so you're not caught off-guard."

"Got it," Paris answered, stepping to the left and proceeding down the hallway. She took two steps and felt the crunch of hard objects under her boot. She was grateful that Faraday had warned her. Otherwise, the sensation would've unnerved her. Then the howling grew louder suddenly, and Paris tensed.

"Someone must've pulled Blood Mary through," Faraday said in a rush. "The howling grows louder when she comes through a mirror."

"Okay, I need to hurry then." Paris picked up the pace, nearly running forward. Her steps must've been heavy enough that they caused a sharp piece of glass to pierce through the rubber soles of her boots and puncture the bottom of her foot. Paris yelped and jumped up on her uninjured foot, grabbing the one that the glass had stabbed.

This threw her off-balance, sending her to the left where she fell into the candle flame and burned her shoulder. The smell of burning hair filled the air. Paris screamed again and rocked forward on both feet. The momentum made her trip and fall straight on her front. She knew that there was broken glass underneath her and her hands were full with the knife and cable, so she rolled forward, out of the move, and popped up—and accidentally, her eyes popped open too from all the excitement.

Hanging squarely in front of her on the other side of the narrow staircase at the end of the hallway, with two candles floating beside it, was an oval mirror with blood streaked down its surface.

"Oh, hell!" Paris yelled, realizing that it was too late for prayers.

CHAPTER SIXTY-EIGHT

Instantly, Bloody Mary appeared on the surface in front of Paris, only a few yards away. The image of the ghost was behind Paris at the far end of the hallway where she'd entered through the window. A piercing howl that seemed to be trying to tear Paris' soul from her body shot through the air. With it was a sharp and chilling wind.

"Oh no!" Faraday yelled at Paris' side.

She had expected that Bloody Mary would crawl out of the surface of the window. That's why she was surprised to see her over her shoulder in the distance. However, that gave her a small bit of hope. Daring to turn around, Paris saw the physical presence of Bloody Mary standing at the end of the corridor.

The evil spirit wore a long white gown. Her stringy black hair hung around her pale face, and like how Paris had been walking through the mansion, she had her head low and appeared to be looking at her feet as she strode forward at an even pace.

Paris glanced at Faraday, hoping he had a way of getting her out of this. Then the howling got even louder, and she jerked her head back up to look at the ghost. Her chin had lifted, and now the blood dripping from her gouged-out eyes was visible. Her mouth was a large gaping hole, blood also dripping from it.

To Paris' horror, with each passing second, the evil spirit was picking up speed, now moving so fast that wind was blowing her hair and gown back.

Paris looked down at Faraday, but she realized that he couldn't see the image of Bloody Mary because he hadn't looked in the mirror. The ghost was coming for her and only her.

"Run!" he yelled, pointing at the stairs, deadly urgency in his voice.

CHAPTER SIXTY-NINE

Clambering over the first few stairs but not tripping, Paris cleared them fast thanks to her demon blood. She did nearly knock her head against the low ceiling that Faraday had warned her about. When she arrived in the attic, she realized it wouldn't be hard to find Mae Ling and Willow. The space was small, and they were only a few yards away. Thankfully it appeared that Wilfred had been able to cover all the mirrors on the wall in the attic.

The headmistress' eyes were wide with horror when she saw Paris running for them. However, Mae Ling seemed as calm as ever, simply waving Paris over.

They'd drawn a large pentagram on the floor in front of them with what appeared to be charcoal. Inside each of the points were different symbols that Paris didn't recognize. She shoved the cable and knife into Mae Ling's hands, then tugged the cilantro from her pocket and gave it to Willow.

"She's coming for me!" Paris yelled, looking over her shoulder, the howling louder.

All the color drained from Willow's face, and she jerked her head back and forth as if looking for an escape hatch for Paris. There wasn't one.

"Don't worry." Mae Ling used the knife to slice through the spool of cable cleanly before dropping it on the floor where it looked like little snakes. She then shoved the knife back at Paris and took the herbs from Willow. "We're almost done."

"What do we do next?" Willow asked, but Mae Ling didn't answer. Instead, she casually sprinkled the herbs onto the pentagram, muttering a spell that Paris hadn't ever heard. She was pretty certain that the fairy godmother wasn't speaking English, but she didn't recognize the language. It sounded ancient.

The howling was nearly deafening.

Paris spun to face the stairs, realizing that she was out of options. She couldn't run any farther. Bloody Mary had her cornered. And they hadn't completed the reverse ritual yet. Hopefully, Mae Ling and Willow could complete it now...but it appeared that this was the end for Paris. There was no getting away.

As she came to terms with this fate, Bloody Mary appeared in the opening at the top of the stairs, her hollow eyes dark and her mouth open wider—her black hair flying back like the wind was assaulting her. The ghost only paused for a moment before floating closer, straight for Paris, one of her hands with bloody fingernails extended as she approached the person she was about to take.

CHAPTER SEVENTY

Paris realized that she was about to die...or go wherever Bloody Mary sent her. The ghost inched in her direction as if savoring the moments before she feasted on Paris' soul. This was it for Guinevere Paris Beaufont, and the spirit seemed to know it as Paris held the serrated knife in her hand, realizing that she couldn't use it against the evil spirit. Her fear was palpable as her hand shook with the knife. That's why Paris couldn't understand why Mae Ling glanced at the stairs and smiled with relief.

"Oh, good." Mae Ling held the spool of cable casually. "We can finish the reverse ritual now."

"What?" Willow asked, horror covering her face as she looked between the fairy godmother next to her and the stairs. She couldn't see Bloody Mary. Only Paris could, but somehow Mae Ling seemed to know that she was there.

"I needed to pull Bloody Mary through to finish the spell?" Paris guessed as the ghost continued to float in her direction.

"No, someone needed to draw her up here," Mae Ling casually corrected like there was no urgency. "It so happened to be you." She pointed at the knife in Paris' hand. "You need to cut your palm...yet again. Maybe the opposite one since the other one is scarred from when you used your blood to grow the Bewilder Forest."

"Huh?" Paris questioned, but then seeing Bloody Mary only five feet from her, decided not to ask any more questions. Instead, she stuck the knife into the top left corner of her palm and brought the blade across.

She didn't know why, but instinct must've taken over because as soon as she'd made the incision, Paris dropped the knife and clenched her palm shut. It was the same as she'd done when she banished the ghost of Hemingway's mother, but this time, she knew it was her demon blood that was the trick.

Of course, she thought as the warm blood dripped from her bleeding palm and onto the pentagram. Smoke rose from where her blood landed.

Bloody Mary froze in front of Paris, an image only she could see. Both her hands shot forward for Paris, reaching for her, but she suddenly appeared stuck in place. Her mouth opened more, now unimaginably wide, as if she was going to swallow a grapefruit whole.

The scream rocked the floor under their feet. It made glass shatter on the floors below. The mirrors too. Smoke filled the attic, originating from the pentagram.

Everything was happening at once so Paris almost didn't notice Mae Ling chanting the spell from earlier beside her. Much like Bloody Mary, she lifted one of her hands and pointed at the evil ghost, although Paris didn't think anyone but her could see her. A moment later, the pieces of cut cables rose into the air and shot toward Bloody Mary, wrapping around her.

The ghost resisted. She fought, screamed, and jerked back and forth. However, none of her efforts worked as the cables wrapped around Bloody Mary like a straitjacket. Before, she appeared to be frozen, unable to close the distance and take Paris. Now she was restrained.

She threw back her head and screamed, her chin back unnaturally farther than it should be as though she was spineless. The scream that rocketed from her mouth was that of nightmares. However, she didn't move, and she couldn't break free of her binds.

Without warning, Mae Ling dropped to a crouched position and slammed the palm of her hand to the center of the pentagram, the smoke partially having cleared to show the floor.

As fast as it had begun, the screaming stopped. The smoke cleared completely. The shaking of the house ceased.

However, Bloody Mary remained, tied up in her binds and her chin back and her mouth moving like she was chanting a spell.

Paris started when Mae Ling grabbed her uninjured hand. She tugged her, walking for the stairs. Willow appeared in shock, not moving until Mae Ling turned and waved her to follow.

"Come now," Mae Ling said, still holding onto Paris.

"B-B-But…" Willow pointed at Blood Mary. "I can see her."

Mae Ling nodded. "So can I and everyone else. She can't hurt anyone anymore. Paris made her solid."

"What do we do with her?" Willow's voice was a hoarse whisper.

"We don't do anything with her," Mae Ling said. "We leave her here. It's where she'll remain, trapped, for all of eternity…well, unless someone releases her. It would be wise to seal the attic and make it off-limits to all…forever."

"She'll live here?" Willow asked. "Is that safe?"

"It's better than her living in mirrors where she can come through to anyone who summons her," Mae Ling stated.

Willow nodded, still gaping at the image of the white and black ghost, tethered by the cables and suspended in the air.

"Don't worry." Mae Ling waved again for Willow to follow her. "She can't hurt anyone like that. The pentagram pins her in place. Paris' demon blood took away the curse that allowed her to haunt and come through mirrors. The wires bind her."

"And the cilantro?" Paris asked.

"It was for good measure." Mae Ling winked. "When in doubt, always add a little spice to your spells."

Paris nodded, allowing herself to be led out of the attic, leaving Bloody Mary in her final resting place.

CHAPTER SEVENTY-ONE

When the fairy godmother mansion started to rattle and the crashing of mirrors echoed around where Whitney Ives was hiding, she knew that she had to leave. The fairy godmothers had figured out a way to trap Bloody Mary, which meant that her plan would no longer work. She'd hoped that the ghost would take most of the dumb fairies—ridding the world of their fake goodness and stuck-up ways.

However, as the floor shook underneath her, Whitney knew that she had to get out. Otherwise, they'd come for her, her cover already blown when the butler identified her. Whitney had heard that much using a spying spell from her hiding place.

The information also told her that Paris Beaufont was the one who helped bring down Bloody Mary, foiling Whitney's plan. She could only hope that she'd done enough damage that the fairy godmothers were broken and couldn't come back from the destruction.

Bursting out of where she was hiding, Whitney found that stupid AI butler stationed in the hallway.

"Stop where you are, Whitney Ives!" he yelled, his tone almost polite with his English accent.

"Fat chance, dip weed," Whitney fired back. Thankfully she'd been smart enough to hide close to an exit. Reversing the trapping spell, she opened the door to the mansion, allowing herself to leave the house where she'd imprisoned everyone using dark magic. Most magicians didn't use the Fang Wellspring because they didn't need it, but her job as a tooth fairy gave her access to it—making her ultra-powerful with both types of magic.

With the mansion still shaking, Whitney bolted out of the house and across the grounds. She opened a portal to Zhuang Alley, where she'd call Courtney and Sidney to meet her.

Unfortunately, they wouldn't be able to return to Loose Teeth College. Headmistress Sham would punish them severely for this. She might not like the fairy godmothers, but mostly that was because they didn't like her. Everyone knew that Headmistress Sham would like nothing more than to mend things with Happily Ever After College. What Whitney had done, unleashing Bloody Mary, well, it would make that nearly impossible.

The three tooth fairy dropouts would be on their own. After this, they'd be on the fairies' most wanted list. The House of Fourteen would be after Whitney since she was a magician. That all meant that they'd have to up their game and develop a way to destroy their enemies.

Most importantly, Whitney wanted to take down the halfling who'd come between her and her friend's plans for revenge. The three rebels would come together, be stronger than ever and make Paris Beaufont pay.

CHAPTER SEVENTY-TWO

The fire in the hearth of Headmistress Starr's office took the chill out of the air that was thankfully dissipating as Bloody Mary's haunting receded into everyone's memory.

Outside on the Enchanted Grounds of Happily Ever After College, the sun was rising, marking a new day. No one had slept much at the college—especially Paris Beaufont. After rounding everyone up and counting the missing, the staff had sent the students to their rooms to try and rest. They'd canceled that day's classes.

The grave expression on Willow's face mirrored the grief in everyone's eyes around the office.

"Ten women." Willow looked at the list of names on the desk before her. "Bloody Mary took ten of our staff and students. How am I going to explain this to their families?"

"You couldn't have prevented this," Mae Ling said.

"But that's the thing," Willow stated with urgency. "The board is going to say this is a result of me following untraditional practices by opening enrollment."

"A magician did this." Chef Ash paced while chewing on the end of his pencil nervously, "but it was because of a grievance between fairies."

"Based on what we've started," Paris began, enjoying the comfort of sitting for the first time in a long time in the comfy armchair, "we're on our way to creating a truce between fairy godmothers and tooth fairies. We're going to have the Fang Wellspring cleaned, which will benefit many, creating much peace. Just think of what will happen to the love meter when there are fewer crimes and problems because of dark magic."

Mae Ling nodded. "What you said about mending relations between the Seelie and Unseelie, well, that's the most remarkable event in several centuries. That alone will have a huge impact on the love meter."

"So although horrible things have happened," Hemingway began, "they weren't avoidable. Hopefully, they will lead to much-needed change. What happened tonight was because of long-standing grievances. It sent you and Paris on a mission to fix these problems, and you will. Unfortunately, three evil tooth fairies took that opportunity to unleash something sinister on the college. But we survived, and we will rebuild."

"We did survive." Christine sighed from her place next to Paris in the opposite armchair. "Thanks to the efforts of some really brave and awesome people."

She and everyone else was looking at Paris.

Suddenly nervous, she coughed and straightened, pointing at Faraday. "He also helped."

The squirrel smiled, his fancy new glasses sitting on the top of his head. "I didn't do much. I certainly didn't bleed to trap an evil ghost."

Paris cradled her bandaged hand in her lap. She shrugged. "I wanted matching scars on both hands so it worked out well."

The group wasn't in a laughing mood, but some smiled when she held up both her hands.

"So will Bloody Mary be in the attic of Happily Ever After College forever?" Christine shivered from the idea.

Mae Ling nodded. "Yes, but she's sealed away."

"I'll keep an eye on her ensuring she doesn't break her bonds and alerting you if she looks close," Wilfred stated.

"They will hold," Mae Ling said.

"Why not kill her and be done with it?" Christine asked.

"Because she's already dead," Mae Ling answered. "She was a ghost who used dark magic to come back through mirrors and rituals. Now, no matter what, she can never return because she's in physical form and trapped."

"That's pretty cool," Christine said in awe. "All because of Paris' demon blood. There's like a hundred and one uses for it."

This made many in the room laugh.

Willow looked like she'd never laugh again, though. Paris leaned forward, offering her a caring look. "I'm sorry that we lost so many people before we stopped Bloody Mary. And I'm sorry that I let Whitney get away."

"That's not your fault," Mae Ling stated at once.

"Yes, she fled before you had Bloody Mary totally trapped," Wilfred replied.

"But she did get away," Paris said bitterly.

"Yes, but there's some good news in this." Willow's tone perked up some. "I spoke with Headmistress Sham before you all joined me. She's expelled the Knees for good. Apparently, they knew that was coming after tonight and had already fled Loose Teeth College."

"I fail to see the good news," Paris muttered. "To get Queen Helena MacGillie to clean the Fang Wellspring, we have to bring her those lawbreakers."

"The good news," Willow continued, "is that Headmistress Sham thinks she knows where the three will go. They'll be on the run. They won't be thinking clearly. She believes they'll hide on Zhuang Alley."

"That evil street where criminals hang out?" Chef Ash questioned.

"That's the one," Willow answered. "I'll alert the House of Fourteen and FLEA to start looking for them. Now that they're actual criminals, it's not only us enlisted to find them. We have all the authorities on the case, so it's only a matter of time before we apprehend them and can turn them over to Queen Helena MacGillie."

Paris sighed and sat back in her armchair, finally relaxing. "That is good news."

"Then the Seelie queen will clean the Fang Wellspring." Hemingway's tone was full of hope.

"Magical races will have clean magic," Christine stated.

"Then the Seelie and Unseelie will quit warring," Chef Ash added.

"And love will have the best chance of blossoming worldwide that it's had in centuries," Mae Ling replied.

"That will be all because of you, Paris." Faraday looked at the halfling fondly.

She couldn't help but smile as she looked around the room of friends. "All because of *us*. None of us do anything alone. We're all in this together. We fought together tonight, and we'll celebrate together when the time comes."

"I look forward to that." Willow rose to her feet behind her desk. She looked around her office, her eyes connecting with everyone stationed around.

"I couldn't ask for a better group to rely on as we face the times that will come. They won't be easy, I fear. There will be more turmoil. I have hope that we'll persevere. Then, when we do, the world will benefit because love will have a chance unlike ever before to spread, as it was supposed to."

Paris smiled, her heart feeling like it was growing in size suddenly. She glanced out at the Enchanted Grounds as the first rays of sunlight peeked up over the trees of the Bewilder Forest in the distance—a new day dawning.

Paris looked forward to the days to come, however hard they would be. All days that brought a chance for more love were good ones. Even if she had to weather storms and fight evil, it was worth it. Making the world a better place was always worth risks and sacrifices.

Ironically, it wasn't because Paris was a halfling that she would potentially fix the wars between the tooth fairies and fairy godmothers and the Seelie and the Unseelie. It was because Paris Beaufont had a tenaciousness to create and spread love unlike anyone in the world.

It was that passion that would lead her into wars that would change the world one day. It was that passion that would make her the greatest peacekeeper. It was that passion that would help her to heal love worldwide.

The halfling was unaware of this and her grand fate as she yawned, exhausted from her adventures, but looking forward to the ones that would come in the days and weeks ahead.

Paris and Faraday and their friends had many adventures in store, and they were all invariably connected to love. It was what made the world go 'round, after all.

SARAH'S AUTIIOR NOTES
SEPTEMBER 10, 2021

Thank you for buying the books, reading them, reviewing them and supporting LMBPN. Thanks for supporting me as an author. And thanks for putting up with my author notes.

Here we go...yet again.

I hope you all never get tired of this part, because it's my therapy. Writing books makes me crazy. Or maybe it's the other way around. Maybe I write books because *I am* crazy. Hard to tell...

Not sure what that says about you...just saying...

I'm going to tell you all a secret now.

Here's what I haven't done in a while: Written a book with another real person around. I write with my daughter in the background all the time. But not a "real" person. I like to think of that little sweet fairy child as a figment of my imagination. However, she doesn't go away when I tell her to.

Anyway, you know what I mean about a "real person." The kind who doesn't have to love me because I pay the bills and feed them and such. That's Lydia. Then there's everyone else...

So the Scotsman visited me...finally...for three weeks. And during that time, I wrote this book. I *think* he still likes me.

You see, when I write, I devote myself to the book. I live and eat and breathe…and you get the point. I sorely hope you get the freaking point. But he had to endure my crazy writing routine and behavior.

It goes like this: Sarah wakes up and spouts ideas. Sarah eats nothing but drinks a lot of coffee. Sarah disappears. Sarah reappears and spouts more nonsense. Sarah does some exercises and drinks more coffee, followed by tea, then water and then maybe something else more questionable. You're not allowed to question. Then Sarah disappears. Magic happens. You all get a book. And then Sarah spouts about all the ideas she's had that she thought were brilliant but wonder if the reader will really like them. Then Sarah crashes. Like really crashes. In mid-sentence…

It's 5 in the morning… Sarah is awake. Let's see if the Scotsman likes the Sarah writing behavior.

Here's what you need to know and maybe Mike can attest to (if he reads these parts of the notes). To write a book means different things for different writers. I immerse myself. I dive in and bathe in that freaking universe. And usually I wake up, sometime later, and wonder where the hell I am and why I have bills from this universe and practical clothes on. And where's the freaking magic, Batman?

But honestly, I don't live in the real world most of the time. I think you might prefer it that way. I read the reviews. I treasure your support. It means the world to me…the world I live in and the one I write about. However, I'm now wondering if others are okay with me living in an alternate universe. Lydia and I have done it for a while and she loves it. She pops into my office regularly or wakes in the morning and says, "Where are we today?" But my question is, when the Scotsman wakes, will he say the same? Or will he be like, why did you crash last night and talk about gnomes and flamingos in your sleep?

I'm going to try and sleep now. But my question to Bird Killer is, what makes you extraordinarily weird? Besides the fact that you kill innocent animals, I mean…

Much love and Peace,

Tiny Ninja

MICHAEL'S AUTIIOR NOTES
SEPTEMBER 23, 2021

Thank you for not only reading this series but these author notes here in the back as well.

Just this once, I should act as if I haven't read Sarah's author notes. That will teach her to stop asking that question in HER author notes.

It's like a Pavlovian Dog experiment. "Let's say Mike doesn't read my author notes, so he has to say something in HIS author notes."

I'm on to you, Noffke... I'm on to you!

So, the question is whether I have something weird about me. Well, there is nothing weird about my sleeping habits and waking up worrying about my partner. My wife has already gone down that route and acquainted herself with the right technology (to cut out the noise) to help her sleep.

It only took about 8 years to come up with the technology solution. There might have been a few choice words between wedding and year eight. Just saying.

Since I've been in a relationship for a while, I imagine all my idiosyncratic rough edges have been sanded off over the years. That's my story, anyway, and I'm sticking to it.

So, in short, Noffke, I am not weird and fantastical as you are. I'm more of a muggle at the moment. Which is kinda sucky, actually. *Maybe we should all just be a bit more Noffke'ish?*

… Dammit, now I have to wait until the next Author Notes to find out what happened w/ the Scotsman. I swear this is just as bad as a cliffhanger in some respects, and Sarah is secretly a diabolical Author Note writer leaving this hanging as she had.

Did he do ok? Did he decide to leave? Tune in next book to find out!

Alright, I see I'm crossing my author notes with Saturday After-noon Matinee movies – it's obviously time to close these down and find a place to take a nap.

Have a good weekend (or week) and talk to you soon!

Ad Aeternitatem,
Michael Anderle

ACKNOWLEDGMENTS
SARAH NOFFKE

I have so many people to thank who make this all possible. Firstly, thanks to Mike, who really pushes me to be a better writer, coming up with the best ideas, not just the really good ones. We work together pretty well, I'd say. I wonder what he'd say… Anyway, MA gave me the opportunity to write with LBMPN a few years ago and it's been life changing. He's very supportive and really cares. Thanks Bird Killer.

A huge thank you to the LBMPN team who work tirelessly so that I have less stress. Thanks to Steve and Kelly for making my life easier and being on top of everything. Thanks to Tracey and Lynne for fixing all my editing mistakes. A big thank you to the JIT team whose feedback at the 11th hour before publishing is invaluable. Thank you to my alpha readers Juergen and Martin. Thank you to everyone who makes getting the books to the reader possible. I really can't do this without you. And you make it so much more fun.

Thank you to my daughter, Lydia, who inspires my stories over and over again. She's my muse and we are always discussing story. She's an avid reader and listens to the Liv Beaufont series at night and reads the Sophia Beaufont books with me before bed. She also reads other authors, which I guess is okay. But my point is that she's supportive of me in so many ways. I need to stay immersed in this universe and remember all the details. There are 12 book in each series so there's a lot to remember. And Lydia loves my stories and then also supports me by listening and reading them so I can keep crafting. But also, she puts up with me when I go all psycho pants during a big crunch of a deadline. I will be the first to admit that I'm pretty intense a day or two before a book is due. And she always just smiles and says, "Mommy, you can do it."

Thank you to my family, the Scotsman and all my friends. You all are always so supportive of me and for that, I'm infinitely grateful. I really couldn't do this without the encouragement of those I love. On the really tough writing days, the Scotsman points out all the things that I don't see, like my dedication to the craft or how much readers are enjoying the books. I don't know what I did to have the most loving and thoughtful people in the world in my corner, but I'm going to do everything to keep them and hopefully keep making them proud.

And finally, thank you to you the reader. Without you I wouldn't be able to do what I love. Your support means so much to me and my family. Thank you from the bottom of my heart.

Love,
Tiny Ninja

BOOKS BY SARAH NOFFKE

Sarah Noffke writes YA and NA science fiction, fantasy, paranormal and urban fantasy. In addition to being an author, she is a mother, podcaster and professor. Noffke holds a Masters of Management and teaches college business/writing courses. Most of her students have no idea that she toils away her hours crafting fictional characters. www.sarahnoffke.com

Check out other work by Sarah author here.

Ghost Squadron:

Formation #1:
   Kill the bad guys. Save the Galaxy. All in a hard day's work.
   After ten years of wandering the outer rim of the galaxy, Eddie Teach is a man without a purpose. He was one of the toughest pilots in the Federation, but now he's just a regular guy, getting into bar fights and making a difference wherever he can. It's not the same as flying a ship and saving colonies, but it'll have to do.
   That is, until General Lance Reynolds tracks Eddie down and offers him a job. There are bad people out there, plotting terrible

things, killing innocent people, and destroying entire colonies. **Someone has to stop them.**

Eddie, along with the genetically-enhanced combat pilot Julianna Fregin and her trusty E.I. named Pip, must recruit a diverse team of specialists, both human and alien. They'll need to master their new Q-Ship, one of the most powerful strike ships ever constructed. And finally, they'll have to stop a faceless enemy so powerful, it threatens to destroy the entire Federation.

All in a day's work, right?

Experience this exciting military sci-fi saga and the latest addition to the expanded Kurtherian Gambit Universe. If you're a fan of Mass Effect, Firefly, or Star Wars, you'll love this riveting new space opera.

NOTE: If cursing is a problem, then this might not be for you.

Check out the entire series here.

The Precious Galaxy Series:

Corruption #1

A new evil lurks in the darkness.

After an explosion, the crew of a battlecruiser mysteriously disappears.

Bailey and Lewis, complete strangers, find themselves suddenly onboard the damaged ship. Lewis hasn't worked a case in years, not since the final one broke his spirit and his bank account. The last thing Bailey remembers is preparing to take down a fugitive on Onyx Station.

Mysteries are harder to solve when there's no evidence left behind.

Bailey and Lewis don't know how they got onboard *Ricky Bobby* or why. However, they quickly learn that whatever was responsible for the explosion and disappearance of the crew is still on the ship.

Monsters are real and what this one can do changes everything.

The new team bands together to discover what happened and how to fight the monster lurking in the bottom of the battlecruiser.

Will they find the missing crew? Or will the monster end them all?

The Soul Stone Mage Series:

House of Enchanted #1:

The Kingdom of Virgo has lived in peace for thousands of years...until now.

The humans from Terran have always been real assholes to the witches of Virgo. Now a silent war is brewing, and the timing couldn't be worse. Princess Azure will soon be crowned queen of the Kingdom of Virgo.

In the Dark Forest a powerful potion-maker has been murdered.

Charmsgood was the only wizard who could stop a deadly virus plaguing Virgo. He also knew about the devastation the people from Terran had done to the forest.

Azure must protect her people. Mend the Dark Forest. Create alliances with savage beasts. No biggie, right?

But on coronation day everything changes. Princess Azure isn't who she thought she was and that's a big freaking problem.

Welcome to The Revelations of Oriceran. Check out the entire series here.

The Lucidites Series:

Awoken, #1:

Around the world humans are hallucinating after sleepless nights.

In a sterile, underground institute the forecasters keep reporting the same events.

And in the backwoods of Texas, a sixteen-year-old girl is about to be caught up in a fierce, ethereal battle.

Meet Roya Stark. She drowns every night in her dreams, spends her hours reading classic literature to avoid her family's ridicule, and is prone to premonitions—which are becoming more frequent. And now her dreams are filled with strangers offering to reveal what she has always wanted to know: Who is she? That's the question that haunts her, and she's about to find out. But will Roya live to regret learning the truth?

Stunned, #2

Revived, #3

The Reverians Series:

Defects, #1:

In the happy, clean community of Austin Valley, everything appears to be perfect. Seventeen-year-old Em Fuller, however, fears something is askew. Em is one of the new generation of Dream Travelers. For some reason, the gods have not seen fit to gift all of them with their expected special abilities. Em is a Defect—one of the unfortunate Dream Travelers not gifted with a psychic power. Desperate to do whatever it takes to earn her gift, she endures painful daily injections along with commands from her overbearing, loveless father. One of the few bright spots in her life is the return of a friend she had thought dead—but with his return comes the knowledge of a shocking, unforgivable truth. The society Em thought was protecting her has actually been betraying her, but she has no idea how to break away from its authority without hurting everyone she loves.

Rebels, #2

Warriors, #3

Vagabond Circus Series:

Suspended, #1:

When a stranger joins the cast of Vagabond Circus—a circus that is run by Dream Travelers and features real magic—mysterious events start happening. The once orderly grounds of the circus become riddled with hidden threats. And the ringmaster realizes not only are his circus and its magic at risk, but also his very life.

Vagabond Circus caters to the skeptics. Without skeptics, it would close its doors. This is because Vagabond Circus runs for two reasons and only two reasons: first and foremost to provide the lost and lonely Dream Travelers a place to be illustrious. And secondly, to show the nonbelievers that there's still magic in the world. If they believe, then they care, and if they care, then they don't destroy. They stop the small abuse that day-by-day breaks down humanity's spirit. If Vagabond Circus makes one skeptic believe in magic, then they halt the cycle, just a little bit. They allow a little more love into this world. That's Dr. Dave Raydon's mission. And that's why this ringmaster recruits. That's why he directs. That's why he puts on a show that makes people question their beliefs. He wants the world to believe in magic once again.

Paralyzed, #2

Released, #3

Ren Series:

Ren: The Man Behind the Monster, #1:

Born with the power to control minds, hypnotize others, and read thoughts, Ren Lewis, is certain of one thing: God made a mistake. No one should be born with so much power. A monster awoke in him the same year he received his gifts. At ten years old. A prepubescent boy with the ability to control others might merely abuse his powers, but Ren allowed it to corrupt him. And since he can have and do anything he wants, Ren should be happy. However, his journey teaches him that harboring so much power doesn't bring happiness, it steals it. Once this realization sets in, Ren makes up his mind to do the one thing that can bring his tortured soul some peace. He must kill the monster.

Note This book is NA and has strong language, violence and sexual references.

Ren: God's Little Monster, #2

Ren: The Monster Inside the Monster, #3

Ren: The Monster's Adventure, #3.5

Ren: The Monster's Death

Olento Research Series:

Alpha Wolf, #1:

Twelve men went missing.

Six months later they awake from drug-induced stupors to find themselves locked in a lab.

And on the night of a new moon, eleven of those men, possessed by new—and inhuman—powers, break out of their prison and race through the streets of Los Angeles until they disappear one by one into the night.

Olento Research wants its experiments back. Its CEO, Mika Lenna, will tear every city apart until he has his werewolves imprisoned once again. He didn't undertake a huge risk just to lose his would-be assassins.

However, the Lucidite Institute's main mission is to save the world from injustices. Now, it's Adelaide's job to find these mutated men and protect them and society, and fast. Already around the nation, wolflike men are being spotted. Attacks on innocent women are happening. And then, Adelaide realizes what her next step must be: She has to find the alpha wolf first. Only once she's located him can she stop whoever is behind this experiment to create wild beasts out of human beings.

Lone Wolf, #2

Rabid Wolf, #3

Bad Wolf, #4

CONNECT WITH THE AUTHORS

Connect with Sarah and sign up for her email list here:

http://www.sarahnoffke.com/connect/

Michael Anderle Social

Website: http://lmbpn.com

Email List: http://lmbpn.com/email/

https://www.facebook.com/LMBPNPublishing

https://twitter.com/MichaelAnderle

https://www.instagram.com/lmbpn_publishing/

https://www.bookbub.com/authors/michael-anderle

BOOKS BY MICHAEL ANDERLE

Sign up for the LMBPN email list to be notified of new releases and special deals!

https://lmbpn.com/email/

For a complete list of books by Michael Anderle, please visit:

www.lmbpn.com/ma-books/

www.ingramcontent.com/pod-product-compliance
Lightning Source LLC
Chambersburg PA
CBHW020421110726
47899CB00006B/2080